GIDEON'S FOG

A JOAN KAHN BOOK

GIDEON'S FOG

J. J. Marric

HARPER & ROW, PUBLISHERS

New York, Evanston, San Francisco, London

A HARPER NOVEL OF SUSPENSE

FIRST EDITION

Designed by Gwendolyn O. England

Library of Congress Cataloging in Publication Data

Creasey, John.
  Gideon's fog.

  I. Title.
PZ3.C86153Ghah [PR6005.R517]   823'.9'12   74–5801
ISBN 0–06–012798–8

1

The Park

TO GEORGE GIDEON, Commander of the Criminal Investigation Department of London's Metropolitan Police, the parks of London were the city's lungs. Take them away, and the eight million or more men, women, and children who lived in the heart and environs of the sprawling metropolis would slowly suffocate. Once, the myriad of houses in the central boroughs and inner suburbs had burned coal, and as the small coal, brought from the deep mines of South Wales and from Scotland, had smoldered and burned, its choking fumes had risen up the narrow chimneys and filled the air with particles of soot and corroding acids.

Not all the smoke had come from tiny houses and small grates; much had come from the larger, more prosperous houses in the heart of the city—in Mayfair and Knightsbridge, Kensington and Victoria. In their huge fireplaces coal had blazed up chimneys once swept—and not so very long ago— by boys whose sweeping brushes had dispersed fumes, which, invisible and unsuspected in fine weather, descended like a blight on the windless days when moisture thickened the atmosphere.

The result was the pea-soupers that silenced and stilled the city.

And killed many by choking them.

George Gideon, on a damp evening in November, realized it was going to be a foggy night, and knew that although fogs were no longer what they used to be, they could be either very bad or very good for the police. If conditions stayed like *this,* it would be bad; the fog would be light enough to allow burglars and pickpockets, bag-snatchers and smash-and-grab practitioners to do their worst and escape in the misty gloom. But if the fog thickened, then thieves and honest men alike would stay at home and the main trouble for the police would be stopping idiot motorists from reckless driving.

Gideon was a big man, massive in every way. As he drove along King's Road and the road gave a little jag, he suddenly was opposite the Eelbrook Common, where nothing appeared to have changed in the forty years he could remember, and he thought back to his boyhood.

On one side of the road the three- and four-story houses—many of them now turned into offices—formed a terrace. On the other side was the Common, only a small open space but one of the city's lungs. Tall trees, leafless after a bitter frost of two nights ago, seemed to be swallowed by the fog. The trees close to the road were solid enough at the base but even their higher, skeletal branches appeared to be fading away. And the fog was thickening. Office workers walking from Fulham Broadway, some holding torches, the beams pointing downward, were already wraithlike figures.

Suddenly Gideon saw what he had never expected to see again; and he could not resist the impulse to pull into the curb to stop and watch, with a huge grin on his face, his mind spanning forty-odd years.

A small figure appeared from behind a tree carrying a candle inside a jam jar suspended by a piece of string tied round the rim. The figure stood near the tree until another figure loomed out of the darkness, moving slowly and uncertainly. Both stopped, talking; then the small figure turned, with the other's hand on his shoulder.

Gideon could almost feel that hand.

There, in that very place, Gideon had often waited on nights as bad as or worse than this, fingers warmed by the gentle heat rising from the candle, waiting until an elderly person, or someone uncertain of the way, came along, then approaching him.

"Can I help you, sir?"

The response had been nearly always querulous. "What, boy? What?"

"Can I lead you where you want to go, sir?"

There would be muttering and grumbling and nearly always a grudging "You may as well. Don't go too fast, mind you."

"No, sir."

Gideon would turn and, with the other's hand on his shoulder, would lead the way over curbs and pavements, past the gnarled trunks of trees, to the person's front door. A penny, and sometimes tuppence, had been his reward.

"Thank you, boy."

"Thank you, sir. Good night."

Gideon would turn and hurry off, perhaps to the same spot, or else to the nearest bus stop where some people were bound to alight. Many, seeing the bus lumbering away, were terrified at being left alone, for one false step would take them into the road, at the mercy of any passing vehicle. With luck, Gideon might get six or seven customers in one evening, and be wealthy for the rest of the week.

A dozen other lads of his age would do the same thing, enjoying the adventure, the sense of superiority over an adult, the sense of earning money. The fogs really *had* been fogs in those days!

All these reflections took only a few seconds, and Gideon's smile faded. He remembered he had called Kate, his wife, to say he was on the way. If he were not home soon, she would begin to worry.

His car was actually moving when he saw the small figure reappear.

He thought, That was quick. The boy couldn't have been gone for more than two minutes, so his patron must have been virtually on his own doorstep. The figure and the candle disappeared behind the tree, and Gideon frowned.

Why should the guide hide from prospective customers?

Men and women, young and middle-aged, some of them mere girls, passed the tree briskly. Then a shadowy figure appeared, hesitated, and stood still. Almost at once the small figure moved forward and there was a consultation before both moved off and disappeared.

The fog was closing in.

There was the stink of smog in the air, too. Cars that had moved at a fair pace were now crawling. More people were walking in groups, one in each group holding a torch and shining the beam round, from walls to curbs and trees. Five buses passed, close behind each other, and on the rear platforms conductors peered to the side, where visibility was better.

A car radio sounded very loud: ". . . and that is the end of the six-o'clock news, but before we continue with our advertised program, here is a message from the Meteorological Office and the Metropolitan Police about tonight's weather conditions. The worst fog of the winter is already causing traffic delays in forty-three counties, and is particularly dense in the Greater London area and London's outer suburbs. Visibility in some places is down to ten feet. All flights in and out of London Heathrow Airport have been canceled, and arriving flights are being diverted to Manchester, Prestwick, and in a few cases to Shannon. . . ."

The voice faded, as if the fog were strangling the speaker.

The ghostly figures on the Eelbrook Common, even those with torches, were moving much more slowly. The candle bearer and his customer were out of sight.

No, they weren't! The smaller figure reappeared, still carrying the candle. This time he had probably been gone for four minutes; certainly no longer. Gideon now had little doubt what was happening. About a hundred yards farther away a pale red glow showed the neon signs of a garage. He moved forward slowly until a petrol sign loomed ahead. He pulled into the approach yard of the garage as a boy in once-white overalls came hurrying.

"Got no more room tonight, mate! Full up to the brim."

"Mine won't be here long," Gideon said. "I am—"

"Can't 'elp it if you're the King of England, mate—you can't stay there." The lad couldn't be much more than fifteen. His bright eyes and cocksure voice proclaimed the very young in authority. Oil smeared his nose and forehead and a corner of his lips.

Gideon opened his car door.

"Well, let's see what you can do for a policeman," he said, and took out his police card.

It was years since he'd shown it; years since he had initiated any investigation into crime. Nevertheless he always kept his card in the outside breast pocket of his jacket, where he could get at it easily.

"A *cop!*"

"A detective, who—"

"Lemme see!" Grubby hands stretched out for the card but Gideon held it safe, merely turning it in such a way that the other could read both the heading—"Metropolitan Police"— and the name of Gideon, with his signature as well as the signature of the Commissioner of Police himself.

"Gideon," the youth whispered.

"Yes."

"I—I used to go to the same school that one of your sons went to."

"And if you keep me standing here any longer you'll prove you're just as dumb as he is," Gideon said, feeling slightly disloyal to one of his sons. He gave the boy a friendly grin, and added, "I won't be long."

He stepped out of the range of the garage light into the fog, and was suddenly in a different world. Forty years ago this might not have worried him, but it did now. He could hear the throb of engines, see pale orbs glowing faintly, hear some engines running fast.

A woman cried out, "Help me! I'm lost!"

A man called: "Stand where you are. Don't move."

This *was* a pea-souper, the old-fashioned kind. The stink was getting worse; the Common was blotted out. A whole blanket of fog had closed in on the area.

Gideon, putting a foot forward carefully, warned himself, "Come on! You can't stay here all night!"

He saw a bus and, finding the curb at the same time, stepped off the pavement into the roadway.

The conductor, just visible, asked in a soft Jamaican voice, "You wish to board the bus, sir?"

"No, thanks," said Gideon.

What kind of fool was he to be in the middle of the road? He walked around behind the bus and peered along in the opposite direction. He could see no lights, no shapes in the roadway itself, but could make out the added density of trees just beyond. He took a dozen steps, kicked lightly against the curb, and a moment later was safely off the roadway.

The fog was a little clearer here, and he saw the spot where the small candle bearer had been. Gideon went across the wet grass toward the path along which people were still walking, many with torches. He could see no one with a candle. He walked in the opposite direction, keeping to the path, helped by the lamps on the Common and the beams of torches. At last, he stopped and turned aboutface.

"Charlie, *don't,*" a girl protested.

A man giggled, out of sight.

Gideon walked on until he reached a street lamp. He put out a hand and gripped the fluted iron post, then leaned against it as if he were exhausted. More wraithlike figures passed.

A youth appeared in front of Gideon, holding up a candle in a jam jar. Gideon saw through narrowed eyes that this was no schoolboy but a youth in his late teens. A peaked cap was pulled low over his forehead, his chin was buried in the upturned collar of his coat.

"You live far, gov'ner?" he asked in a high-pitched voice.

"No," Gideon answered, speaking agitatedly. "No, only a few streets away, in Lime Avenue, but—but this fog—"

"Like me to show you home?"

"Oh, if only you would! But how can *you* see? What chance have you—"

"I know this place like I know the back of me hand," the

7

youth interrupted. "Put a hand on my shoulder, guv, and trust me. What number Lime Street?"

"Seventeen."

"Have you there in a brace of shakes," the youth assured him, and started off at a reasonable pace. He crossed the path, then walked along to the Row which faced New King's Road, where traffic moved like a trail of ghosts. Then he turned a corner to the right.

Gideon, still missing steps but very alert, saw torches and the shadowy figures of two men loom forward from the doorway of a house; and he knew at once that they were coming to attack him. As the thought flashed into his mind, the candle bearer wriggled free while the other two men closed on Gideon. He saw the weapons in their hands, saw their arms drawn back to strike.

*

2

Captives

NEITHER OF THE ATTACKERS was large, and Gideon was huge, but he was supposedly bewildered and scared by the fog, and so should have been an easy victim. He saw the speed and sensed the viciousness with which the men sprang.

It was a long time since he had been in a fight.

Now he was not only wary but furiously angry. Instead of swaying backward to avoid the blows, he heaved his great body forward. His clenched fist caught one man on the side of the jaw with a force that first rocked him sideways and then felled him. The other ducked his head and, dodging a blow, brought his knee up toward Gideon's groin. Gideon made a half-turn, took the knee on the bony part of his thigh, then flung the other man backward. The man staggered, gasping, missed his footing, and fell.

"If you try to get up, I'll break both your necks," said Gideon.

They stayed on the ground.

"What happened to the other people you attacked?" Gideon demanded.

"We didn't hurt them," one of the men said sulkily.

"So you just robbed them and pushed them off into the fog."

"They—they weren't hurt, I tell you!"

"They'd better not be," Gideon said.

The fact that none of the victims was nearby suggested that the man was telling the truth; but at least two—and probably several more—who had accepted the offer of help were now wandering about, lost, robbed, terrified. There was nothing Gideon could do about it at the moment, and he had another anxiety. There was no sign of the third fellow, who might have run off while the going was good, or might be circling round to attack. He would probably have a weapon. Gideon glowered down at the two captives, as a car engine sounded and a horn honked. Several cars, lights dimmed, turned in to the street, led by a youth with a lantern.

One of the men on the ground muttered, "Give us a break —we won't do it again."

"You never said a truer word," Gideon growled. "Your next stop will be the police station, even if I have to drag you there by the scruff of your neck."

But that was more bravado than anything else. He needed help to carry out his threat, and even if he could put out a call it might take a patrol car an hour to get here, if it arrived at all. His own car was much handier. If he could get them home, he could lock them in the garage until a patrol car came for them. And the bank of fog was lifting; he could even see the garage across the road.

"Now get up," he ordered the men. "One at a time, back to me." He waited for the first man to rise, took his right wrist, and held it behind him; if he tried to run, a slight upward thrust would cause enough pain to stop him. "You next," he said to the other.

This man sprang to his feet and darted off, but Gideon, ready, shot out a leg and tripped him. The man sprawled again, as the first man gasped, "You're breaking my arm!"

"I won't break anything if you do what I say. Take two steps to the right."

The man took two shuffling steps. His companion had obviously jarred himself in his second fall and was sitting up looking dazed. A little group of people turned the corner. Before Gideon could call out, a man approached from the narrow stretch of Common between the main road and the garage. Seldom had Gideon been so glad to see a policeman's helmet. It bore down on Gideon purposefully.

"Do you need help, sir?"

"Yes," Gideon said. "I want to get these two on a charge as soon as I can."

"There should be a patrol car across by the garage soon, sir."

"Good," said Gideon. "Get that chap to his feet, and we'll go to the garage. Did you see what was going on?" he asked, hardly able to believe that possible.

"Oh, no, sir." The constable, small-boned but strong, was dragging the second captive to his feet. "The boy at the garage told me he thought you might have spotted something. I just came to check. What *did* happen, sir?"

"We need a third man, who was offering to guide people home in the fog, leading them round the corner," Gideon said, "and robbing them with the help of this pair."

"Did they try that on *you*, sir?" The constable smothered a laugh.

"They tried it on me," Gideon asserted dryly. They were halfway across the narrow strip of grass now. His hold on his

11

prisoner was firm, and he was about to ask questions when he kicked against something. The policeman shined his flashlight downward.

It revealed a jam jar with a piece of string tied round it, and a candle loose inside.

"That could be our third man's," Gideon said. "Pick it up by the string," he told his prisoner, "and don't drop it. How many people did you attack?"

"About—about six. But we didn't hurt them, I swear it!"

Six, eight, ten—it didn't greatly matter to begin with; there must be an immediate search for all of them. The prisoners must be closely questioned, to help make sure all their victims were found. By the time they reached the garage, Gideon knew exactly what to do. The boy attendant was coming out of the storage area at the back, oilier and more bright-eyed than ever.

"So there *was* something up!"

"There was something up," Gideon agreed. "Thanks for your help."

Swelling with gratification, the boy started talking.

He was still talking when the police car arrived. At sight of Gideon, the two plainclothesmen in it scrambled out and stood almost to attention, with the boy and the two captives looking on. Gideon spent no more than three minutes telling them what to do, and before he left they were busy at the walkie-talkie radio. Organizing a search was not going to be easy, but if a dozen policemen covered the streets beyond the Eelbrook Common it should not be long before any people wandering, lost and frightened, were found. Once he was satisfied everything was in hand, Gideon moved to his own car, carrying the jam jar by the string.

"Who the hell *is* he?" demanded one of the prisoners.

"You don't know him?" cried the lad who had tried to

move Gideon on. "Why, everybody knows *him*. That's Gideon of the Yard. You know—Gee-Gee."

"Gawd," groaned the second prisoner. "And we thought it was our lucky night!"

Police Constable Arthur Simpson was at the extreme end of the Metropolitan Police scale from Gideon, who was the senior executive, subordinate only to the Commissioner.

Arthur Simpson had been on duty alone for only a week; in actual fact, he was the youngest man in the Force in terms of service. He had, of course, an extensive period of training behind him; he had been out with other constables, older men used to the job. He was fully trained and lacked only experience.

Unlike Gideon, he was not a native Londoner; his parents had brought him to London when he was very young, and had moved to Fulham. They now had a house out at Wembley, and he still lived at home with them, although he had a married sister who lived in Fulham, where he could spend a night if he was too late to catch the last bus or underground train. Tonight his sister would expect him.

He was already off duty, and had been when the boy at the garage, young Alfie Tate, had told him about Gideon. No one would have guessed at the turmoil in his mind as he had crossed the road, or the wild beating of his heart when he had actually set eyes on Gideon. It had been an astonishing sight, Gideon holding one man in a powerful grip, with the other man dazed and on the ground. He, Arthur Simpson, would never know how he had managed to keep his voice calm.

"Do you need help, sir?"

Instead of glaring, or uttering some instant command, Gideon had said calmly, "Yes. I want to get these two on a charge as soon as I can."

13

It had been the tone of voice, the complete acceptance of him, Arthur Simpson, as competent to help that had steadied Simpson; and there was the heaven-sent knowledge about the patrol car. After that it was just a job of work; he had accepted Gideon as completely as Gideon had accepted him. Not until the Commander had driven off had a reaction set in, and now all he wanted to do was sit down. And laugh. He could see the great Gideon getting into the car and holding the jam jar as if it were full of tadpoles or something as precious.

"What's funny?" asked one of the patrol men, coming from his car.

"Er—nothing."

"Well, I'll give you something to laugh at. The Super wants you at the station to tell him what the prisoners were up to, and after that he wants volunteers to go looking for the poor old granddaddies lost in the fog."

"I'll volunteer!" Simpson said eagerly.

So, early in his career, he explained exactly what he had seen and done, promised a full report in writing in the morning, saw the two prisoners locked in the cell at the Fulham subdivisional station. Then, fortified with cocoa, sausages, and mashed potatoes, he had joined another man and set out on his rounds. He would have liked the Eelbrook Common area; instead, he was sent to North End Road. The fog, although not so impenetrable as it had been, was still thick and smelly, but far less traffic was about. Most of the public houses, the clubs, a picture palace, and some discothèques were quiet; even the young people, once home, stayed indoors. The two policemen found a drunken man, and then later an elderly woman, who was at the front door of her house just behind North End Road, peering up and down the street.

"Can we help you, Ma'am?" the older policeman asked.

"I don't know what to do," the woman said. "My daugh-

14

ter's husband hasn't got home, and she's frightened of staying by herself, and the buses don't seem to be running."

"Where's your daughter live?" asked the policeman.

"In Putney. It isn't far from the bus stop once I'm there. I'm sure I could find my way, but—" she broke off.

"There are some buses still running," the older man remarked. "We'll walk with you up as far as Fulham Road. You can catch the next one that comes along."

"Oh, I'd be so grateful!"

Walking with an old woman whose daughter was scared, helping Commander Gideon—what a night! Arthur Simpson thought. All his training had told him how varied his job would be, but what a night! He heard the woman talking in a monologue which needed no responses. A cat appeared out of the mist, miaowing; could *it* be lost? A dog barked, another howled. They reached a bus stop and had not been waiting more than a minute before a bus came up, its red paint partly discernible in the lifting fog.

"Putney Station and then the garage," the conductor called, hanging half off the bus.

"The station is just right for me," the woman said eagerly. "Oh, thank you, Constables, thank you ever so much!"

"We made *her* happy, anyhow," the older officer said, and as he spoke his transistor radio beeped. He switched on to "speak." "P.C. Coleman answering. . . . What? . . . Oh, bloody good! . . . I'm with P.C. Simpson—okay for him, too? . . . Right, I'll tell him." He switched off, taking his time, obviously testing Simpson's patience before he divulged: "We're finished for the night. No need to report to the station. But don't expect that every night, Simmy. Usually they make you report back even if the heavens are falling."

"Sure I shouldn't have spoken to them myself?" asked Simpson.

15

"Don't you come it, sonny. I'll tell you what you have to do. Going to try to get to Wembley?"

"No. My sister's place," Simpson replied.

"Where's that?"

"Near the Chelsea Football Ground."

"You go your way, I'll go mine," said P.C. Coleman. "Good night."

"Good night," Simpson echoed.

The fog *was* better but it certainly hadn't gone. The street lamps, the car headlights as they came forward, the torches— all had a halo about them, giving the night a kind of beauty.

He couldn't explain why, but he wanted to go back to Eelbrook Common, to the spot where he had seen Gideon. It would take him another half-hour, although if the fog kept on thinning he might pick up a bus. He took a number of side streets until he was at Fulham Broadway, deserted even at the entrance to the underground station, then approached the Common from the northern, broader end. Before long he was on the path Gideon had taken. He thought of the people who had been victimized. The crafty, cold-blooded devils, promising to lead them home, then robbing them.

He went to the very spot where he had seen Gideon, and stood quite still. In the distance he heard a bus engine. Then, a moment later, almost at his side, there was a moan. He stiffened, and looked toward the long terrace of houses with their small gardens. The moan was repeated, coming from a garden in front of one of the houses. He opened the gate and flashed his torch. The beam fell on the pale face of a gray-haired man who lay on his side. As the gate squeaked and Simpson went toward him, the old man moaned again.

3

One Major Crime

GIDEON PUT HIS CAR, a large black Rover, into the garage round the corner from Harrington Street, Fulham, where he lived, and walked briskly to his house, less than a hundred yards. He carried the jam jar carefully. Each old-fashioned street lamp had its own ring of mist; most of the front-door fanlights of the houses, which held the street numbers painted on them, glowed with light. His was no exception—43. It was too misty to see the small neat front garden or the red, white, and blue tiles of the path, laid by some patriotic builder about the time of the Boer War, but there was a faint reflection from the white-painted front door.

Kate had wanted the door white, and although he would have preferred a darker color, tonight he was glad it was white. He unlocked the front door, but before he had opened it, Kate approached from the kitchen.

"Is that you, George?"

"It's a hungry copper," called Gideon.

"I was afraid you'd be late," Kate said as she came along the passage at the side of the stairs.

It was difficult to say why there were some moments when her impact on Gideon was much greater than at others. She always moved well, a tall and well-formed woman whom some called statuesque; she always dressed well, if conservatively; she made up a little, never too much; and her dark hair invariably seemed as lovely as it was luxuriant, cut well by a good hairdresser, and clustered about her head. Perhaps her anxiety put fresh radiance into her gray eyes; perhaps a little of the fog had crept into the old house, misting and softening her features. Certainly there was something.

"Hallo, love!" Warmth resounded in his voice. "Am I very late?" "Late" he meant compared with the half past six he had promised when he had telephoned from the office, not late as such; in periods of intense activity at the Yard he was lucky to be home before midnight.

"Not very," she said. "What on earth are you carrying in your hand?"

He held it to one side, kissed her lightly, then held the jam jar up.

"A jam jar," he stated unnecessarily.

"Even I could see that."

"A very special jam jar," he assured her. "Shall I tell you now or wash and tell you while we have dinner?"

"Tell me at dinner," she decided. "You won't be long, will you?"

"Ten minutes."

"That'll be just right. We'll eat in the middle room, dear," she told him, and hurried away.

He carried the jam jar carefully into the room they called "middle." This was now a combination of living room/dining room when the family were at home, and television room. He went upstairs, washed in the big old-fashioned bathroom, with its colorful patterned tiles, and changed to slippers and a comfortable jacket.

It was a particularly quiet night.

Was that only because of the fog and the fact that few people were moving about in the street? And few cars? Or was it the house, which seemed so empty up here? He had a sudden and unwelcome change of mood, almost one of depression. It *was* empty these days, with all the children gone, or so nearly gone it made little difference to the household.

And once there had been six children!

Once, there had been almost seven—

"This won't do!" he said aloud, and started downstairs. Yet he stopped and looked back at the room from which he had just come. There, twenty years before, Kate had lain in childbirth, begging him not to leave her; but there had been an urgent call from the Yard and he had left, with a neighbor in attendance and a doctor on the way.

The child had died, and she had blamed him.

For a long time afterward there had been great tension between them and he had thought the marriage would break; but for the other children, it would have, for she had so hated and resisted his dedication to his work.

He reached the foot of the stairs, and an aroma of roast beef —or could it be mutton?—came along the passage. It was beef!

"Can I help?" he asked.

"If you'll bring the sprouts in, and the gravy, I'll bring the Yorkshire," Kate said. "You can carve right away."

He sharpened the carving knife on the steel that had been in use for thirty years—it had outlived two sets of knives and forks—and cut into the meat. He carved generously in thick slices.

"Perfect!" he said, and she lowered the Yorkshire pudding to a heat-resisting mat.

The Yorkshire was just as he liked it, tempting enough to warrant a second helping. Gideon ate with single-minded attention, tackling the following apple pie with almost as much zest. Presently he sat back with the air and look of utter repletion.

"My, that was good!"

"It must have been," Kate said, pleased. "You haven't said a word about the jam jar."

"And I'm not going to until you tell me what occasion I've forgotten."

"You haven't forgotten anything as far as I know."

"No anniversary?" Gideon mused, marveling. "No child's birthday? No grandchild's? It seemed a rather special effort."

"You're right, darling, it was a very special effort. Priscilla and Peter were coming for dinner but didn't, because of the fog!" Priscilla was their second daughter.

"What a shame," Gideon said. "Were they in town?"

"Yes, this morning, but as the fog closed in they decided to go back early. I was in the mood for cooking, anyhow. Now I won't wait a moment longer—what is the story of the jam jar?"

He told her. . . . And it led to reminiscing; of the days when he had guided people home and the fact that she had had a brother, long since dead, who had earned coppers in the same way. Even Malcolm, their eldest son, now thirty and with three children, had followed in his father's footsteps, but by the time his own sons had been old enough the really bad pea-soupers had gone.

It was an evening of "I remember, I remember."

As he sat and talked, Gideon forgot almost everything to do with work; but when he switched on the television for the ten-o'clock news, he was jolted back to the crimes on Eelbrook Common, fascinated by stories of the fog that was now spread over three-quarters of the country. Shipping, air, and train services were at a standstill, very little traffic moved on any roads. After a fifty-two-car pileup on the M-1, heading north, all motorways in the area were closed.

"Will it affect you much?" Kate asked as they went upstairs to bed.

"Shouldn't think so," answered Gideon.

He was sure that if anyone had used the fog as a cover for major crimes, he would be told about it. But he didn't really expect many crimes.

He was right.

In a bad fog the real professionals stayed at home. A few small-time criminals burgled houses near their own homes. Some who had been planning to leave the country by air, with stolen jewels or currency in their baggage, had to sweat it out at the airports. Others did what the two men Gideon had caught had done: preyed on the elderly groping their way home.

There was, in fact, only one major crime in London that night, a murder which the murderer believed would never be discovered.

His name was Robert Marriott.

He was a married man of thirty-four, with an attractive wife and three children, the oldest nine, the youngest two.

He was an unusually good-looking man whose smile lit up the whole of his face, and could set many a girl's heart beating fast.

It had stopped one girl's heart from beating at all, over a year ago, and *that* body had never been discovered, so why should this one? For his killing he needed fog, thick, impenetrable fog, and he had been waiting for such a night as this for months, nourishing a hope that had grown into impatience as November came and still there was no fog.

But last night there had been some, and the forecast was for more, and much thicker, tomorrow: which was now today.

So he had telephoned Mary.

"Hallo, darling!"

"Oh, Bob—it *is* you!"

"Yes, darling, it is your old friend and lover, Robert the Marriott."

"Bob, where are you?"

"Where do you think I am?"

"I hope you're in London," Mary had said.

"And for once your hopes are vindicated," he had told her. "The fog is a blessing—I can't go north."

"You mean—you're *free* tonight?"

"Free as I shall ever be."

"Oh, darling, that's wonderful!"

"It will be, if you're free, too."

"Oh, I can be, I—Bob! Everyone's talking about leaving early tonight because of the fog. I could get away by four o'clock."

"Four!" Robert Marriott had echoed with apparent enthusiasm. "It really is our night, sweetheart, because I can get away soon after three. Don't speak, let me think." In fact, he knew exactly what he was going to say. He could picture her with her young, round face and her pretty blond curls and her slightly swelling stomach, where their child lay so snug and warm. "I've got it!" he said at last, as if he had made a great discovery and a great decision. "I'll be at the entrance to the Cumberland Hotel at four o'clock."

"Oh, darling, be inside. It'll be warmer!"

"All right!" he promised. "I'll be inside, but—you'll have your coat, won't you?"

"Of course," she said, puzzled. "Why?"

"Because I want to go for our usual walk," he said. "I'd hate to miss a stroll through the park."

"Oh, that will be lovely," she replied eagerly. "I just don't want you standing about. I could be held up at the last minute."

"Try not to be," he had urged. "And I've a surprise for you!"

She had not kept him waiting for a single minute. She had come in wearing a close-fitting hat and a scarf and a loose coat so nondescript that no one would possibly recognize her by it. Nor would they recognize him, for he had a false beard and mustache, which made him look so different that although she saw him, she didn't recognize him. Disappointment was heavy on her face when she made a complete circle of the foyer, and passed close to him.

"I told you I had a surprise for you," he had said.

He could see her now, spinning round, eyes radiant at the sound of his voice, then clouding, then glowing again as he stretched out his hands.

"Bob, you've grown—"

He had not allowed her to say more, but had taken her in his arms. Anyone who saw them would have guessed they were lovers who had been parted for a long time. Arm-in-arm they went out of the hotel across streets where visibility was poor but not dangerous, into the park—Hyde Park—where they had done their lovemaking in the long, warm summer nights.

Where he had done other lovemaking.

The fog had been very thick here.

23

The strange thing was that, knowing what he planned to do, he could still feel desire for her. As strange, that in the thicket where he took her the fog and cold seemed to melt away. He spread his raincoat for a sheet, and her coat over them. It was not strange that he should fondle her, and caress her neck, and she did not suspect what he was about to do when at last his hands tensed to a killer grip. She gasped when he twisted; but that was all.

Soon he opened his briefcase, took out tools, and began to dig the hole in which to bury her.

The topsoil was rich and loose; even the shrubs were easy to pull up. He removed four, then used a large trowel to scoop out the undersoil, which was gravel for several feet down. It was heavy work, and he sweated so much that drops fell down his face and onto the earth.

Once, he thought he heard a footstep and his heart seemed to turn over.

He stopped digging, got up on one knee, and listened intently, but the sound was not repeated. For a few minutes he was very cautious, constantly raising his head to listen, but gradually he began to work faster, until he was satisfied that the hole was large enough.

He lifted Mary's body, lowering it carefully, tucking in the sprawling limbs. It was not long before it was partially covered. He rested for a while, listening but hearing only distant, mournful sounds. When he started again, he dug into gravel he had not disturbed before. It was surprisingly loose, and for this he was thankful, until his trowel struck something hard and metallic. Puzzled, he dug farther.

At last he cleared enough gravel away to make out the shape of a box.

He thought, *Someone's buried that!* And he stared in horror. *They'll come back!* He was suddenly panic-stricken, for if whoever had buried the box came back for it, they might find Mary's body. For a terrifying moment he thought, *I must dig her up, take her away!* But even in the fog he dared not do that.

If he left the box there and they found it, they would not worry to dig deeper.

He shoved the dark soil over the gravel and covered the box again, and, gasping for breath, replanted the shrubs. No one would be surprised to see the soil disturbed about newly planted shrubs. What mattered was to get away. He cleaned his tools and put them back in his briefcase, then shook the raincoat free and folded it; he could throw that away later.

Once outside the shrubbery, he peered in all directions, but there was only the fog. He walked away, trying to prevent himself from hurrying.

4

Bright Morning

IT WAS STILL DARK when Gideon woke. Kate was breathing the regular, deep breath of healthy sleep, and he lay on his side for a few minutes, relaxed, and remembering. Then he pushed the bedclothes back cautiously and got out of bed, noting that the hands of the bedside alarm clock pointed to ten past seven. An early morning at the office would do no harm. He had a quick shave, a tub, and was dressed within twenty minutes. Creeping down the stairs in his slippers, he congratulated himself that Kate hadn't stirred. As he reached the telephone extension in the hall, he heard the faint *tok* of sound that always preceded a ring, and snatched up the receiver.

"Gideon," he said quietly.

"That was quick," said a Cockney voice, and Gideon recognized it as the voice of an old friend and colleague, once his chief aide, now a superintendent at N.E. Division, one of the roughest in London. "Good morning, George!"

"Good morning, Lem. What's your trouble?"

"Me? Trouble? Never let it be said!" Lemaitre was in a

light-hearted and happy mood, not the easiest to bear with early in the morning. But Lemaitre would not call him at home unless there was a good reason. "You heard the rumor?"

"What rumor?"

"A great big London copper was seen going home with a jam jar full of tadpoles."

"Only they weren't tadpoles," Gideon retorted. He was surprised that the story had got around so quickly, and wondered who had started it. "What's on your mind, Lem?"

"That jam jar," answered Lemaitre.

"Lem, this is no time to—"

"Sorry, George," Lemaitre interrupted hastily. "But if it has the fingerprints on it I *think* it has, then I'd like to get it tested and checked early."

"I'll take it to the Yard. Why the hurry?" Gideon wanted to know.

"Because the man whose dabs are on it, if I'm right, is a nasty piece of work named Sparrow Smith, and I want Sparrow on several jobs and I'd like him inside on a week's remand. He's planning a trip," added Lemaitre. "I had a tip that he bought a ticket to Rome last night and is still at the airport. I'd like to pick him up before he leaves, and the planes are beginning to fly again."

"I'll have the jam jar picked up, taken to the Yard, and have Fingerprints call you," Gideon promised.

"Thanks," said Lemaitre. "I called them first, thought you may have sent it in already. Meanwhile Old Bill at Heathrow is keeping an eye on Sparrow for me. I've got nothing on him, George, but we can delay him long enough to have those prints checked." After a moment's pause, Lemaitre asked with a laugh in his voice, "What does it feel like to be out on the beat again?"

"Good," answered Gideon. "How—" He broke off, for he

27

could ask questions later. "Lem—you call Information and have them pick this jam jar up, will you? It will be ready in five minutes."

"Right-ho!" Lemaitre, still apparently on top of the world, rang off, leaving Gideon shaking his head.

He put the jam jar into a shoebox and was sticking down the lid as a police car pulled up. Gideon went to it as the passenger opened the door.

"Don't get out," he said. "Take this to Fingerprints at the Yard immediately."

"We'll see to it, sir. Good thing the fog's cleared, the roads are a mess."

That was the first time Gideon realized that the fog had gone completely, and it was noticeably colder. He wondered what kind of mess the roads were in as he went back to the kitchen and made himself some tea. He would get breakfast at the Yard, he decided, and could be on his way soon after eight.

As he drove along New King's Road, he understood the patrol-car man's remark. Cars were stranded, some in, some on the curb, some on the pavement, some dangerously far from the curb. Bicycles lay about, too, where their riders had simply given up. A few motorists were already starting their cars; others were getting off buses and walking toward their stranded vehicles. This would be happening all over London, of course. But if he knew London, Uniform, and the Traffic police, the roads would be normal by midday, and if fog hadn't returned there would be no trouble tonight.

He wondered why Lemaitre wanted Sparrow Smith and if the man who had escaped last night was indeed Smith. Drawn by some compulsion, he turned off the main road to the one on the other side of the Common. On the pavement close to the spot where he had been attacked was an old-fashioned leather cosh, flexible, filled with lead shot, capable of knocking a man out with one blow—capable of killing if the blow was hard enough, and yet leaving practically no superficial sign of injury.

He got out and picked it up by the thick end, looked about and noticed nothing more until, back at the wheel, he saw something glisten beneath the street lamp, the light of which was fading in the coming dawn.

The glistening thing was a watch glass, unbroken. It might have nothing to do with what had happened here last night, but he put it with the cosh on the seat next to him, and started off again. He was back on New King's Road when he saw two police cars, one with two detectives from the Fulham subdivision, turn off toward the Common.

"Wonder what they're after?" he asked aloud.

He was held up at traffic lights at the extreme edge of the Common and, looking about, noticed a big, badly written sign fastened to the trunk of a tree. The lettering, in red and blue, was smeared from the damp, but the message remained, clearly visible: "CLEAN UP OUR PARKS."

The lights changed, engines roared, the man behind Gideon honked a "Get a move on" protest, and Gideon moved on. Traffic, swollen by much that came from Fulham Broadway, was now so thick that he had no chance to ponder.

It took him half an hour to reach Parliament Square, nearly another ten minutes to get to Scotland Yard. Everything here was normal. As Gideon mounted the long flight of stone steps, the air echoed with "Good morning"'s. He passed a dozen Japanese in a group in the hall, one of the parties of police from overseas that had long been a feature of Scotland Yard, noticed a tall, strikingly attractive young woman obviously waiting for something or someone, then strode on to his own office. This had two windows overlooking the Embankment

29

and the Thames. A desk, armchairs, filing cabinets, and a table made up the furniture.

His desk was bare but for three telephones and the trays fastened to it, marked, "Out," "In," "Pending," "Typing Pool." He was surprised, for usually it was spread with reports of cases already vetted by Alec Hobbs, the Deputy Commander. Hobbs was still a widower, and usually in early. What would happen to his punctuality after he had married Gideon's daughter Penny, Gideon couldn't imagine, for she was a concert pianist whose work kept her up late at night.

Where *was* Alec?

Gideon reminded himself that he was earlier than usual. Alec was probably in his own office, next door, going through mail and papers. Gideon gave a loud warning cough, and opened the door.

Hobbs wasn't at his desk; his hat and coat weren't on their stand.

Gideon frowned as he approached the pile of unopened letters on Hobbs's desk. Unless there was something very urgent, it would probably be better to leave everything untouched, but there were some pending investigations he was anxious to follow up quickly. He was sitting on a corner of Hobbs's desk, turning the letters over, when he heard his own telephone bell ring. So he lifted this one.

"Put the call from my room through here," he said to the operator.

"One moment, sir—you're through."

"Commander?" It was Lemaitre again, but less informal.

"Yes, Lem?"

"We got him," Lemaitre announced with great satisfaction. "Sparrow's dabs were on that jam jar, couldn't want anything clearer, so we've got him. George—"

"What?" asked Gideon into a pause.

"You'll see he's remanded in custody for a week, won't you? I need a week to check the other jobs I want to prove against him."

"I can't see anything but an eight-day remand and we'll oppose bail," Gideon promised. "Where is he now?"

"On the way from Heathrow to Fulham."

"Good. Lem—how did you hear about me and the jam jar?"

"Cor lumme, it's everywhere!" Lemaitre exclaimed. "Some bright spark put it out on the teletype last night—hasn't Hobbs shown you a copy?"

"He's not in yet," Gideon replied.

"Alec's not? Homer nods, after all! Well, I can read it out—"

"Don't worry, thanks," Gideon said, and went on: "Did you have much trouble last night?"

"Not so much as usual," Lemaitre assured him, "except"— there was a laugh in his voice; Gideon had seldom known him in a brighter mood—"the Enemies of Loving Couples have been at it again."

"You're talking in riddles this morning," Gideon said, trying not to sound too gruff and disapproving. Lemaitre had always had the ability to get on his nerves.

"Riddles? Hasn't Alec told you about Elsie?"

"Lem, I haven't time to waste," Gideon said sharply.

"Er—sorry, George." Lemaitre was always quick to withdraw from a position of danger. "What I mean is, some of the bushes in Hyde Park were cut down and others were pulled up by the roots last night. The bushes are love nests, if you know what I mean, and the Enemies of Loving Couples, or Elsie, are doing quite a job of destroying the nests. Yes, sir! Quite a job." Lemaitre suddenly adopted an atrociously bad American accent, while Gideon saw in his mind's eye a sign with the colors running into each other, reading: "CLEAN UP OUR PARKS."

"What kind of a job?" Gideon asked.

"I've told you. If they have their way, there'll be no rolling in the hay in Hyde Park again, no cover-up for illicit passion. You mean Alec *hasn't* briefed you about what's been going on?"

"Not yet," Gideon answered.

"Biding his time," Lemaitre opined sagely. "He's a deep 'un. And how's the affair between him and Penny coming along?"

"The way love affairs usually come along," Gideon answered, somewhat heavily. "That is, the church-bell variety." Penny was twenty-six, Hobbs over forty and a widower; and Gideon visualized a fairly early wedding.

"Good!" replied Lemaitre heartily. "Penny always was the apple of my eye. Well, thanks for the jam-jar job, George! Anything else you want me for?"

"Not now," Gideon answered shortly.

He rang off, and stared at Hobbs's empty chair. Why hadn't Hobbs told him more about this vandalism in the parks? For whatever the cause and no matter how morally justified the perpetrators believed themselves to be, it *was* vandalism.

Should he make a note for Hobbs and leave it on the desk? No, he decided; next time they were talking, he would bring up the subject, if Alec didn't get it in first. He probably would.

There was one major investigation he and Hobbs had in hand, a serious one. It dealt with a number of jewel robberies, mostly from private houses but with a fair sprinkling from dealers. Only the most valuable jewels were stolen, and at first the inquiries had been routine: each case had been followed up; a description of the jewels was circulated not only through-

32

out Great Britain but to most of the world's police forces. After a while it was thought that the crimes were linked. None of the stolen jewels had been recovered either by the police or by the insurance companies.

Six months before, in this room, Hobbs had said, "I'd like to put one man on the investigation, Commander. It looks as if it's a well-organized series of burglaries; no matter how quickly we visit the fences, we never find anything."

"Good idea," Gideon had agreed. "Who've you got in mind?"

He could remember Hobbs's faint smile even now, as if Hobbs had anticipated Gideon's reaction when he said, "Spruce Bruce."

"Must we?" Gideon had said.

"Do you know, George," Hobbs had said, dropping formality—a rare thing in the office—"I think Nathaniel Bruce is the only man here you've ever really shown prejudice against."

"Hope I've not made it public knowledge."

"No one thinks you dote on him," Hobbs had said dryly, "but I suspect you keep the strongest of your reactions for me. Has he ever upset you?"

Gideon had pursed his lips, as he pursed them now.

"Not by any specific thing, no. His manner somehow gets under my skin."

"A bit hard on him," Hobbs had suggested.

"I shouldn't have thought so. He's a first-class man, seldom misses a trick, and has a very good record of arrests," Gideon said. "Any dislike I may have for him is hardly likely to hold him back."

Now, after six months, there was no progress; only a much longer list of victims, so that every so often a newspaper ran

33

an article asking why Scotland Yard was allowing so much license to jewel thieves. The case had become a kind of running sore.

Here on Hobbs's desk was a handwritten note: "Would be grateful for an early interview. N.B." The loops were very exaggerated; there was something almost feminine about the writing. Gideon, mindful of his talk with Hobbs, dialed Bruce's number.

Immediately there was a response in a rather high-pitched voice: "Superintendent Bruce."

"Gideon here," Gideon said briskly. "Mr. Hobbs has been delayed. Do you want to wait for him, or see me about your note?"

"I'd like to see *you,* sir. The sooner the better."

"Then make it now. I'm in Mr. Hobbs's office," Gideon said, and rang off.

If Spruce Bruce lived up to his reputation, he would not be long; and before Gideon had been able to do more than look through some recent notes on the jewel robberies there was a tap at the door and the Superintendent came in. He was a dapper man, immaculately overdressed in a neo-Edwardian suit. His dark hair was plastered down with some kind of scented hair pomade. He had a waxed mustache, which curled up stiffly. Under long eyelashes his brown eyes had the shiny brightness of a chestnut fresh from its husk.

"Good morning, Commander. The Deputy isn't sick, I hope."

"I don't know what's delayed him," said Gideon, and went on without preamble: "What's so urgent?"

"*I* think it urgent and I'm sure Mr. Hobbs would. I hope you will agree, Commander." If this was an attempt to ingratiate himself, it wasn't very good. "A man was picked up in Hyde Park last night. He drew attention to himself by running

34

away when he saw two of our men who were taking a party of Yugoslavs across to the Albert Hall. He slipped, and was picked up, as I say. He had *these* with him."

Dramatically, Bruce thrust his hand inside his pocket and drew out a wash-leather bag. The neck was untied and Bruce allowed a cascade of diamonds to fall from the bag onto his palm. They scintillated brightly in his hand.

"The diamonds stolen three weeks ago from Leet & Son in Hatton Garden, sir," Bruce stated. "I've checked size, carat weight, brilliance, and color. No doubt at all. It *looks* as if the prisoner had either hidden the bag under some bushes, as there are particles of soil in the folds, or dropped them in the dirt at some stage."

"Could be," Gideon agreed. "What do you want to do?"

"Well, with your permission, sir, I won't report to Leet & Son just yet. We've got this man and he may talk—so far, he won't give his name and he *says* he found the bag on the ground. What I would like to do is consult my brother, sir."

"Brother?" echoed Gideon, startled.

"Yes, sir. My brother—whom Mr. Hobbs has met over the Elsie nuisance—is Controller of Parks. Both of us desired when at school to enter some kind of public service, and he, being a born gardener, took a post in Saint James's. He's worked himself up to Controller, sir—the parks mean as much to him as the police force does to me. He will be able to say where the dirt on the bag came from, and—he'll give us every possible help, I'm sure."

"I'm sure he will," echoed Gideon mechanically. "Go ahead."

"Thank you, Commander!" Bruce, as pleased as a child promised a new treat, turned like a dancer on the balls of his feet and went out.

Gideon watched him leave. It would be impossible to find

a more enthusiastic and dedicated officer; it was a thousand pities there was something about him Gideon didn't like. He shrugged, and turned to the other files. The most important was about a six-month-old bank raid. One of the men known to be involved was still free but there was a whisper that he was in London, though this morning had brought no further report and no major crimes had been reported during the night.

He heard his telephone ringing again and this time went into his own office to answer it.

"Gideon here."

"Oh, Daddy!" It was Penelope—a rather breathless Penny. Gideon had the strangest flash of percipience: that she and Alec had got married, had jumped the gun, had—"Have you seen Alec this morning?"

"He's not in yet," said Gideon, tremendously relieved.

"I can't understand it," said Penelope. "He didn't call me after the performance last night, and he nearly always does. I'm in Liverpool," she added as an afterthought, "and we're playing tonight again. There's no morning rehearsal, so ask him to ring me at the hotel before half past one, will you?"

"Yes," said Gideon.

"Bless you! I wouldn't worry you at the Yard unless I were —well, I don't understand it," Penelope repeated, and without another word she rang off.

Gideon, putting the receiver down slowly, did not understand it either, but there must be a simple explanation: Hobbs had been held up somewhere by the fog. Yet trying to convince himself of that wasn't easy; he could understand Alec being held up but not his failure to telephone Penny, or his failure to telephone the Yard. Now it was half past nine: very late for Alec Hobbs. It was much too early to be worried, of course, and yet Gideon was uneasy. Moreover, his routine was disorganized: Hobbs usually vetted all the cases under review and discussed them with Gideon, but one could not wait indefinitely.

He sent for six superintendents in charge of pending cases. The oldest was Jim Danson, close to retirement at fifty-five; the youngest Alan Banning, who, at thirty, was one of the youngest Chief Detective Superintendents at the Yard. He was the only one who made no reference to a jam jar.

Finally, Gideon closed the door on the last of them. He wanted to see the jam-jar telex piece, and was about to go into Hobbs's room to make a thorough search for it when his telephone rang.

"Gideon," he said gruffly.

"Sorry to worry you, sir," a man said. "It's Reception here. There's a lady who had an appointment with Mr. Hobbs at nine o'clock, and she's still waiting. Mr. Hobbs doesn't seem to have come in yet."

"Who is she and what is her appointment about?" asked Gideon.

"She is a Miss Hilda Jessop, sir—spelled with an 'o-p.' And she says Mr. Hobbs knew what it was about and it's difficult to explain in a few words."

"Oh, all right, bring her along," Gideon conceded. It was half past eleven and she had been kicking her heels for a long time. Where was Hobbs? This was so unlike him.

Gideon was at the window looking onto the rare November spectacle of a sunlit Thames when there was a tap at the door. On his "Come in," it opened and the lovely woman he had seen earlier was ushered into the room.

5

More of "Elsie"

SHE WAS REALLY LOVELY; a true platinum blonde with silvery-gray eyes, a perfect complexion, and an unusual regularity of feature. She might be a little too perfect, and might lack some animation—but no, there was feeling in her expression as she came forward.

"Miss Hilda Jessop, sir," announced the police constable from Reception, and went out, closing the door quietly.

"Good morning," Gideon said. "I'm sorry you've had such a long wait."

"It is so unlike Alec," she replied.

The way she uttered the name suggested familiarity; it could imply that she had come to see Hobbs on personal business.

"Very," Gideon said dryly. "Do sit down."

"Thank you." Like Kate, she had a natural grace of movement; and she had an attractive figure and slim, nicely shaped legs. Her shoes, like her gloves, were impeccable. "Will he be much longer, do you think?"

"I've no idea," Gideon said.

"You mean he isn't out on an assignment?" She sounded incredulous.

"Not to my knowledge," Gideon replied.

"Then what on earth can have happened?" Her pleasantly modulated voice rose in what seemed to be genuine concern. "I took it for granted—but I should have known better," she diverged, as if vexed. "Alec wouldn't stand me up like that."

Again there was that hint of familiarity.

"Alec wouldn't deliberately keep anybody waiting," Gideon said shortly. "Is this visit a personal one, Miss Jessop, or is it a police matter? If official, I may be able to help."

She hesitated for a long time before answering. "It is official, although I first talked to Alec about it as a friend." She adjusted the hem of her skirt, then suddenly went on with a rush, "It has become urgent or I wouldn't have worried you."

"What is urgent?" Gideon asked.

By now, he had a feeling that she was being deliberately evasive, was teasing him with obscure comments to hold his attention, and he did not like anyone, not even a beautiful woman, using such tactics on him. He had another anxiety. This woman *might* be very attractive to Hobbs—attractive enough to make him break his engagement to Penelope.

Was he being a fool?

"So he hasn't told you about me," she said.

"Not a word," replied Gideon.

"Ah, how like him," she said with a smile. "He told me he would say nothing to anybody until we'd met this morning. I— Commander, I *think* I am in danger of my life."

The words came out flatly, each one sharp, cold, clipped. Her expression seemed to freeze; so did her body. Gideon did not know whether to groan in dismay, or take her seriously. People who believed themselves under threat were daily callers at the Yard. But this young woman seemed to mean exactly what she had said, and yet she watched him as if knowing that he doubted her.

"And was Mr. Hobbs investigating the circumstances?" asked Gideon.

"Yes."

It began to add up. She was a friend, possibly a friend of a friend, and Hobbs had been inveigled into promising to help; had, perhaps, made some inquiries. Hobbs would be as wary as Gideon of anyone who seemed to have a persecution complex, but if this woman had some kind of claim on him, he might well have promised to investigate. He would keep the story from Gideon, not want to harass him with what might prove to be a trivial affair.

"And he was to have told you this morning what he had discovered?" Gideon encouraged.

"It was to be a *quid pro quo,*" Hilda retorted. "I was to tell him what *I* had discovered also."

"You know," Gideon said, leaning back in his swivel chair, "I hate to admit it but I really haven't the faintest idea what you are trying to tell me."

"Alec and I made a deal," she said sharply.

"About what?"

"The parks."

"The *parks?*" Gideon ejaculated.

"Yes. You must have heard of the campaign to clean up London's parks and gardens. You *must* have." She eyed him intently. "You surely know that there are people who behave with such promiscuous indecency in the parks that others no longer feel it possible to walk through them. As I told Alec, the attitude of the police is one of the most shameful aspects of a shameful situation."

"Oh," said Gideon. "And what is the attitude of the police?"

40

"Utter indifference," Hilda Jessop replied. "It is difficult to believe they have not been instructed to turn a blind eye to what goes on. Young people sprawl in the grass, even close to the paths, in the most shameful of attitudes, and as for what goes on in the bushes—"

"Bushes!" Gideon had a swift mental picture of Lemaitre, and a momentary illusion that he could hear the Cockney voice, saying: "What I mean is, some of the bushes in Hyde Park were cut down and others pulled up by the roots last night. The bushes are love nests, if you know what I mean, and the Enemies of Loving Couples, or Elsie, are doing quite a job of destroying the nests. Yes, sir! Quite a job."

"What kind of bargain did you strike with Mr. Hobbs?" Gideon demanded curiously.

"A very simple one. He wanted to know who was damaging the bushes and thickets in the park, a form of vandalism which he told me is on the increase. I promised to find out, if I could, whether any of the militant organizations were responsible."

"Women's militant organizations?"

"Mostly," Hilda Jessop admitted.

"Did you find out?"

"I think I might have some clues."

"Such as . . ." Gideon began, and paused hopefully.

"I really don't intend to give information away without learning anything in return," the young woman retorted. "Alec promised to find out whether there is any directive to the police to turn a blind eye to what goes on. *Is* there, Mr. Gideon? *Is* there? Surely you must know, if anyone does."

Gideon studied her for what must have seemed a long time, and she didn't look away; her directness was not far removed from boldness, and she was demanding an answer. Gradually he felt anger rising: against this woman and her attitude, her —was "arrogance" the right word? He leaned forward, placing his large hands palm downward on the desk.

"Miss Jessop," he said, "causing damage to public property can be a serious offense, punishable in certain circumstances by imprisonment. Any person or persons withholding information from the police about such offenses are virtually conniving at their continuance. If you have such information, I want it, here and now, please."

She was completely taken aback by his change of attitude; and she was far from the first person to be deceived by his mild and easy manner. He was, in some circumstances, granite hard; and in others, ruthless. He was first and last a policeman, allowing nothing to stop him from maintaining the law. Now he looked not only massive but powerful as he stared stonily at the young woman before him.

"*Now,* please," he repeated in an unrelenting voice.

"I don't know—" she began.

"If you came here with information for Mr. Hobbs, you can give it to me," he interrupted. "Do you know who is responsible for the vandalism in the parks, Miss Jessop?"

She scarcely moved her lips as she answered, "I—I might."

"Please don't play with words. Do you or don't you?"

Gideon wondered whether he was goading her into stubbornness; he did not think she was an ordinary woman and was sure his change of approach had caught her off balance. He wished he knew more than the little Lemaitre had told him.

Suddenly, she was defiant: "I *think* I know. I'm not sure."

"We can soon make sure."

"*Have* the police orders to turn a blind eye to what goes on in the parks?" she demanded, and her voice cut like a knife.

"No," Gideon replied.

"If you are lying to me—"

"That is more than enough," Gideon interrupted icily. What on earth was the matter with Alec to allow himself to make any kind of agreement with this woman? He pressed a bell for a messenger, then dialed Information. "There was a teleprinter message last night about a man with a jam jar," he said. "Send me a copy, will you?"

"Yes, Commander," the man at Information replied.

Gideon grunted "Thanks." At the same time, there was a tap at the door and an elderly police constable appeared.

"Officer, take Miss Jessop to the front door," Gideon ordered, "and if she has a car, see that she has any assistance required."

"Very good, sir."

"Commander—" began Hilda Jessop.

"You will be hearing from us more formally," Gideon said coldly. "Good morning."

She stood up slowly. There was a regality about her, a kind of imperiousness which the circumstances could not disguise. Then she moved, reminding him vividly of Kate.

"Good morning," she said, and followed the older man out.

Gideon waited until the door was closed, and then dialed Reception; a man answered and Gideon said, "You brought a Miss Jessop to my office just now. Have you got her address?"

"Yes, sir."

"What is it?"

"Just one moment, sir." There was a rustle of paper, and then the information came: "41 Meybrick Crescent, Knightsbridge, sir."

"Thanks." Gideon jotted the number down and then sat back. Questions seeped into his mind. Had he used the right tactics? And would there be any harmful effects if he hadn't? Why had he felt so angry? He was used to all kinds of insults and accusations; the "if you are lying to me" had had an effect far greater than the words themselves justified. And why had

43

this haughty young woman waited so long for Alec Hobbs?

Where *was* Hobbs?

He called Information again, and the same man answered him.

"Gideon," Gideon said. "Have you had any word from or about Mr. Hobbs this morning?"

"No, sir."

"Put out a feeler or two," Gideon ordered. "Nothing official, but check the nearer hospitals and—but you know what I want as well as I do."

"Commander—" the man began.

"Yes?"

"Do you think he might have been injured?"

"He's absent, and he's sent no message," Gideon replied. "At this stage I don't understand why. There may be a perfectly normal explanation, so be discreet."

"I'll handle everything myself, sir."

"Good," Gideon grunted. He rang off, and for a thoughtful moment beat a tattoo on the desk. Then he lifted the exchange telephone, said "Get me Fulham," and rang off. Almost at once the door opened and a young constable with fair hair came in. Eyebrows and lashes of the same pale color made him look almost like an albino. He carried a single sheet of paper, which he brought forward nervously.

"From Inspector Cowliss, sir, of Information."

Gideon took it, nodding dismissal, then read:

To all Divisional H.Q. and substations. Information is required as to the whereabouts of John, known as Sparrow, Smith, aged twenty-seven, height five feet two, weight about seven stone, hair medium-coloured, eyes slate-grey. Smith is wanted for questioning in relation to robberies from elderly men who were offered guidance in the fog in Fulham (Eelbrook Common area). Two men have been charged at Fulham subdivisional station with assault and robbery. Both men, names appended, were arrested by Commander George Gideon on his way home from the Yard last night. It is reported that a jam jar, containing a candle, is missing from the scene.

Gideon gave a snort of a laugh; the implication was obvious, and if this would give the Force some light relief, it would do more good than harm. He looked at the telephone: the call to Fulham was taking a long time to come through. On that instant the bell rang and he picked it up.

"Gideon."

"You're calling me, sir. Fulham substation?" The speaker had a husky voice, perhaps due to nervousness.

"Have those two chaps picked up on Eelbrook Common gone to court yet?" asked Gideon.

"Yes, sir. And we asked for an eight-day remand. Superintendent Lemaitre is sending a third man, John Smith, who'll be up this morning, too."

"That's all right," Gideon said. "Who's giving evidence of arrest?"

"Police Constable Arthur Simpson, sir—the officer who was with you."

"Let me see a copy of his report," Gideon said.

"Which one, sir?" the other man asked.

"Which one?" Gideon repeated sharply. "Are there two?"

"Well, yes, sir, I gave him instructions to make separate reports. After he had come in with the two prisoners, sir, he went out on extra duty—nearly everyone did—and on his way home he found a man in a garden close to the place where the arrests were made. The man had minor head injuries, but they had serious repercussions, sir. He died in hospital from a seizure only two hours ago."

6

Hobbs

GIDEON FELT A SHOCK run through him at this unexpected news, and realized that he was remarkably sensitive this morning. He must get hold of himself.

"I'd like both reports," he decided crisply.

"Very good, sir."

"Does it look as if the seizure was brought on by the attack?"

"It could have been, sir—the police surgeon's report isn't in yet, and of course the body hasn't gone to the morgue."

"Right. Send me the reports through Division in the usual way."

"Yes, sir."

"Another thing," Gideon said. "Do you know who put up the 'Clean Up Our Parks' sign on the Eelbrook Common? I noticed it last night."

"Oh," the subdivisional man said, "that was Elsie."

"*Who?*"

"I—er—I—Elsie, sir. It's a nickname we gave to a commit-

46

tee which is trying to—er—stop canoodling and suchlike carrying on in the parks. Elsie's just the nickname for the Ecology of London Committee. E.L.C., sir, sometimes known as Enemies of Loving Couples.''

"I see," said Gideon heavily.

"Glad I could help, sir.''

The man rang off almost too quickly, and Gideon wondered who he was, why he should be so nervous. He would have a word with the Superintendent of Fulham Division; or, better, get Hobbs to have a word. Hobbs. For a few seconds he had forgotten that Hobbs wasn't in the next office. He resisted a temptation to go in and check, and pondered on the fact that "Elsie" had been on the tip of this man's tongue, so the nickname was far from new—except to him, Gideon. Why had Hobbs kept it from him? For that matter, if it was such a commonplace nickname why hadn't he heard it from a dozen sources? He liked to think that there wasn't much he missed.

He put in a call to Fulham Division, but the Superintendent in charge was out. He left word to be called back, and then concentrated his thoughts on Alec Hobbs. There had been a time when he had been wary of the man. It could have been because he came from a public school and King's College, Cambridge, an educational background unique at the Yard. At first Hobbs had been unpopular, yet he had risen quickly on sheer merit. Gradually it had dawned on Gideon that Hobbs was an utterly dedicated policeman who had joined the Force because he believed so absolutely in the need for a strong and efficient police force.

Today he was one of the most respected men at the Yard. His wife had been ill for many years before finally fading out of life. The effect on Hobbs had been to drive him with even greater compulsion into his work at the Yard. For a while he had made enemies, but gradually the tempo had slackened, and his colleagues had begun to understand the hurt that goaded him.

How long ago that seemed.

Then, two years ago, Gideon had discovered that Hobbs was in love with Penelope, and Penelope seemed to be falling in love with him. And now Gideon was daily expecting to be told the date of the wedding. So the Hilda Jessop matter couldn't be serious.

Yet who was the lovely woman who had come to see Hobbs, a woman who was obviously a friend, and one who came from a background much nearer to Hobbs's than Penny's. Nonsense! Gideon told himself.

True, at a date yet to be specified, Hobbs was to be promoted to the post of Assistant Commissioner for Crime, which would make him—nominally, at least—senior to Gideon. But Gideon had been offered the post and had refused it, and had recommended Hobbs, who could give the job fifteen years, at least, while Gideon could give it no more than three or four.

Gideon pushed his chair back and stood up. He was very hungry, and had missed breakfast; it was too late now, but a mixed grill in the cafeteria would put that right. He was at the door when the telephone rang. Hobbs? He strode across and picked up the receiver.

"Gideon."

"There is a Miss Jessop on the line, sir."

"Oh," said Gideon. "I'll talk to her." He waited for a minute, and then said, "Miss Jessop?"

"Commander, I am sorry if I was rude when I was in your office," Hilda Jessop said. "I feel strongly about the subject, I'm afraid, but that is no excuse. I am not sure who is responsible for the vandalism in the parks, which I find as abhorrent as their use as brothels. However, I do know that some fanatical members of the Ecology of London Committee have sworn to take the matter into their own hands, on the basis that if there are no places where couples can count on semi-privacy, then there is less risk of shocking behavior. This was what I had intended to tell Alec."

Gideon, who had already recovered from the sound of the name which was now becoming so familiar, said mildly, "I'm most grateful. Thank you."

"You are kind not to be angry," she said. "Is there any news of Alec?"

"No, but I've no doubt we'll have word soon."

"I do hope so," she said, and added: "Please give him my" —there was the slightest of pauses before she added—"regards."

"Be sure I will," Gideon promised, and almost immediately a thought flashed into his mind. "Miss Jessop, does the word or the name 'Elsie' mean anything to you?"

"No," the other replied thoughtfully. "I have a friend whose name is Elsa, but otherwise no—should it mean something?" She sounded intrigued.

"No reason at all," Gideon assured her. "Goodbye."

Although he was so hungry, and although he had been on the way to the canteen, he crossed to the window. A faint haze covered the Thames, and as he stood there Big Ben began to chime: it was half past twelve, and a lovely day.

Where *was* Hobbs?

And how well did he and Hilda Jessop know each other?

At last he turned, one decision at least come to. If there was no news when he got back to the office, he would have to start a serious search for his chief assistant.

Deputy Commander Alec Hobbs was only two miles away from Scotland Yard at that moment; he was slowly, very slowly, coming round from a long period of sleep or unconsciousness. At that stage he was not aware which. He could not even remember the crash, or the people who had run toward him.

Robert Marriott looked up at the hazy blue sky, and smiled. He was driving along the motorway toward Birmingham, where he lived. He would see Ruth, his wife, tonight, and their older child might still be up, although the others would be in bed and probably asleep.

He had to report at his office at two o'clock this afternoon.

He was a salesman of office machinery and equipment, with a wide territory, and virtually his own boss. Yesterday, before the fog, he had taken an order of over twenty thousand pounds' worth of adding machines and typewriters.

He could look forward to a very prosperous future.

And he could make a fresh start now that Mary was gone.

His smile broadened. What a pretty little thing she had been! But what a brainless one. He could almost hear her, now: "Don't worry, darling, there's nothing to worry about. I take pills."

But a few weeks later: "Darling, I—I think I might be going to have a baby."

And a few weeks later still: "I *am* going to have a baby, Bob. You—you will get a divorce, won't you?"

Why were they all the same? Well, nearly all. He had known one or two who had believed in sex for fun and had looked after themselves, and yet—now he came to think—they had left him because of other men. They must have realized he would never break up his marriage, and had gone off with more eligible chaps.

He gave a sudden bark of laughter; it took hold of him so completely that his wheel swerved—not wise when he was driving at eighty-five miles an hour. Slow down, Roberto! He

50

slowed down and gradually controlled the laughter, although occasionally a gust would burst out of him, as if through a leaky valve.

He had never thought of the possibility before, but—

Supposing the girls who had married other chaps had carried *his* babies to their marriage beds.

God! What a joke!

And what a scare he had had when he had found that box!

Suddenly, his engine missed; picked up, missed again. He scowled, braked, stopped the car, jumped out, then flung up the hood. He heard another car stop and a man ask, "Want any help?"

"Be glad if you can tell me what—" began Marriott, without glancing round. He heard the man draw nearer; and then was aware of an excruciating blow on the back of his head.

With the second blow, he died.

Mrs. Prendergast looked at the policeman at her front door, and did not know what to say, she was so frightened. Not of the policeman: hers was a blameless life, as was her husband's. But what was this young man doing here? She had reported Cyril was missing, had telephoned the police station soon after daylight, and a man with a loud vibrant voice had taken down her name and address, and Cyril's name, and the address of the offices in the City where he worked. He had been in that one company's employ for over fifty years, and for over fifty years had come home on the District Line, walking across the Eelbrook Common.

It was the same house he had always come to.

At first they had rented one room and shared the bathroom; then they had taken over the top floor—all three rooms *and* the bathroom. Eventually they had bought the house, owned it, and brought up two children, both now dead. And finally they had let out the upstairs because the cost of living kept going up, and they couldn't expect the firm to keep paying more; it was a miracle they kept him on.

The young policeman looked rather pale; and too thin. Undernourished.

"Mrs. Prendergast?" he asked.

"Yes."

"Mrs. Prendergast, I'm afraid I have some bad news for you."

She gripped the side of the door, and suddenly felt as if the floor were giving way. But for Police Constable Arthur Simpson, she would have fallen. He was aware of a younger woman on the stairs, a heavy, flabby-faced creature wearing a blue apron and pink, feathery slippers.

"Can you help, please?" Simpson asked her, suddenly authoritative.

Soon Mrs. Prendergast was on the old-fashioned button-upholstered sofa in the front room, its dark red a strange contrast to her white face. Once he knew she was comfortable, Simpson had to tell her why he had come: break the news that her husband was dead; tell her there had to be a formal identification.

He was not sure whether she heard him; she looked as if she were made of wax in which deep lines had been cut by a sharp instrument.

"She hasn't got a living relative, poor soul," the woman from upstairs said. "But I'll look after her." She moistened fleshy lips. "I *could* save her the awful need to identify him. *I*'d know him in a flash," she said. "He was such a nice old man."

"Jessie," William Retford said to his wife, "if Mary isn't home by dark tonight, I'm going to tell the police." He was a short, fat man, manager of a grocery store in Tottenham, a district in North London.

"Will, dear—"

"It's no use 'Will, dearing' me anymore," Retford interrupted. "She goes out far too often and stays out too late. You've no control over her at all, and it's time I put my foot down."

"But, Will, dear—"

"*You* say she has told you she's staying with friends when she stays out all night, but I'm not so sure," Retford interrupted again. "I think you're in league with the girl to pull the wool over my eyes. Well, there's going to be an end to it. If she's not back by dark, I'm going to report her missing. And if she's found in compromising circumstances with some man, *I'll* take control in future."

All Mary's mother said was "All right, Will."

How could she tell him that Mary was going to have a child? How could she or Mary even hope for understanding from him? Hope, if there were any, was that the child's father would marry her, but Mary had never talked of him, and still lived in a world of fantasy.

She had stayed out all night as she'd done often recently, and hadn't gone to the hairdresser's shop where she worked. Mary's mother had telephoned the salon, and learned that. And when Mary did come back, there would be the even greater worry: what to do about the unborn child.

That was the very moment when Alec Hobbs woke again, this time with a clear mind.

He could remember everything; and was appalled.

Earlier that day, a Jamaican lad named Lennie Sappo knew some moments of terror.

He liked being on his own, climbing trees, exploring. And he liked finding his way back on foot from various parts of London. On the night of the great fog, he had been in the grounds of a house in Cricklewood, where there were some apple trees with fruit still hanging on the leafless branches. The "FOR SALE" notice was still up, and he had expected to have the garden to himself, but suddenly he had heard a heavy motor engine. He had dived through the thick shrubbery, and seen a van backing up the drive.

He had seen the driver open the double doors at the back of the van; and had seen him drag another man out, a man whose hands were tied behind his back.

"If you try any tricks," the driver had snarled, "I'll bash your head in."

Lennie Sappo, terrified, had turned and crept back through the shrubbery, and made his way slowly, fearfully, back to Notting Hill.

He told no one.

In the crowded house and the crowded streets where he lived, one minded one's own business, and did not get involved with the police.

7

Attack

UNLIKE GIDEON, Alec Hobbs had no early memories of London pea-soupers; smokeless zones were already common in his boyhood. In any case, what time he had between school and university he preferred to spend at his parents' country home, and rarely visited their house in Mayfair. So a thick London fog was not only an experience but a kind of adventure for him.

But he knew the problems it created for the Yard's Traffic Division, and the problems it might cause the C.I.D. The forecast was so bad that on the previous day he had decided to make a round of divisions where cases were pending. This would cost only his time, instead of that of a half-dozen senior men; it would give him a chance to look in at the divisions and so familiarize himself with their districts.

He had told Gideon what he proposed to do, and Gideon had simply said, "Don't get lost in the fog."

That *was* a possibility, and Hobbs intended to be back at the Yard by half past four at the latest. If he got the information he expected, he would talk to Gideon for the first time about "Elsie." The whole affair had seemed so ridiculous at first that he had taken little notice of it, and but for Hilda Jessop he might not have probed very deeply—if indeed "deeply" was the word.

He simply asked about the Ecology of London Committee in passing. Most of the Superintendents and Chief Inspectors he talked to knew of it as a bee-in-the-bonnet group who wanted to clean up London's parks. Few knew very much. One or two laughed and asked, "What's Elsie been up to now?" No one took it seriously: a few shrubs cut back or uprooted in some of the smaller parks; a few badly printed signs. That was about the limit of it, or it would have been but for Hilda.

He had known Hilda Jessop much of his life, but had lost touch with her in the last few years. He believed she had taken a post abroad. She was well-off, he knew, the only daughter of parents who had died young. As a teen-ager, she had spent some holidays with his family, but he, being ten years older, had not had much to do with her. Beyond wondering vaguely over the years why she had not married, he had virtually forgotten her; until about two months ago.

She had called him at his flat in Eaton Square one evening.

"Why, Hilda! How nice to hear from you."

"I do hope you mean that, Alec."

"Of course I mean it. Why shouldn't I?"

"I've been hearing so much about you," she had said. "You are a great policeman now, aren't you?"

"Well, a policeman."

"Alec the modest, as always. And I'm told you're going to get married again."

"Yes," he had said, with quiet firmness. "Later this year."

After a pause she said, "I'm so happy for you! I—I didn't know Helen had—had died."

"Some years ago," he had told her.

"I am so very sorry." She paused again. "Alec, you will *never* guess why I called you."

"I hoped it was for old times' sake."

"That, of course, and something else."

There was no point in making a wild guess, so he had simply said, "Do tell me, Hilda."

"I want your help as a policeman."

"Good lord!"

"May I come and see you?" she had asked, almost pleadingly. "It's not a thing I can chat about over the telephone."

"I don't quite understand," he had replied.

It had been late—well, lateish, but there were strong ties of family and friendship with Hilda which he could hardly ignore. Nevertheless, he had felt doubtful, perhaps a little uneasy.

She had always been an intense person. She had always come straight to the point, too, and had that night. She told him she was working, voluntarily, for an organization which was helping unmarried mothers. The society was bitterly opposed to abortion; it provided facilities for young women to go abroad and have their babies, helped with money, and was entirely confidential. The members then found homes with good families for the unwanted infants. At this stage, Hobbs had wondered how he could be expected to help—unless some of the girls were being blackmailed, which would not be surprising.

Then she had said, "I have been told that if I do not stop this work, I will be killed."

"Oh, nonsense!" Alec Hobbs had said.

She had sat staring at him for a long time, and he had gone on awkwardly: "I mean, no one in their senses would threaten to kill you for doing work like that."

"Yet I have been threatened," she insisted.

"You have actually been warned to stop?"

"Yes."

"How? By letter? By telephone? Do you know who it was?"

"It has always been by telephone," she had replied. "No, Alec, I don't know by whom. That is what I hope you will find out for me." He could picture her, shivering suddenly; see the change in her expression, the hardness in her eyes. "Is that too much to ask of an old friend?"

"No," he had said, and repeated emphatically, "No." Then a thought had flashed into his mind. "There's something you can do for me in return."

"Must I repay you?"

"Not for me personally," Alec Hobbs had said, "but the police. Do you know a group called the Ecology of London Committee?"

She had not hesitated: "Yes."

"I want to find out whether it is responsible for the present spate of vandalism in the parks," Hobbs had told her. "Uprooted bushes and so on. Finding that out isn't the easiest thing to do." Before she could interrupt, he went on: "We could put a policewoman spy among them but we don't particularly want to do that. Do you think you could help us?"

"I'll try," Hilda had said.

"Now I need to know more about the society you work for, and whom you've been helping and when the threats began."

Even as she had told him, he had begun to wonder whether she was suffering from a persecution complex. Ever since he could remember, she had felt that the world had treated her badly; and in a way it had. She had been an only child, for instance, and lonely; there had been the blow of losing her parents; an engagement in her late teens had been broken off. Had she gradually come to see enemies in the shadows? Could she possibly want to draw attention to herself? The society she had joined was a nebulous one, a group of people, mostly Roman Catholics, working together but without a tight organization.

He hadn't known much about it on that first night.

He did not know very much about it now, two months later. True, he knew the names of some of the other members and of some of the girls who had been helped, but that was all. And he had found nothing to prove that Hilda was under threat, or that any of the other members of the society had been threatened. And meanwhile Hilda had brought him no information about Elsie.

He had asked her to come to see him at the office for what he meant to be a showdown.

Tomorrow morning?

Was this the day of that crash; of the women who had run not to rescue but to attack him?

He had been at the wheel of his own car, a white M.G., chosen because it was more easily visible in darkness and in fog. He had made his last visit to the Hampstead district, where they knew all about Elsie and were highly amused by her; or had been at first, although now the local authorities had begun to get worried. If, in fact, the damage to the shrubberies and bushes was not the work of individual vandals, as they had at first supposed, and Elsie or any organized group was behind it, then it had to be stopped, quickly and ruthlessly.

By then, darkness had fallen and the fog was very thick.

Hobbs cautiously turned a blind corner which he knew well; and then, without a moment's warning, a black van seemed to shoot straight at him. He had practically stood on the brake, but the crash had come. At least he had lessened the force of impact, and had been braced to take the shock. He was shaken but not hurt.

Then, from the back of the van, three women had come running, and behind, two more.

My God!

One of them had wrenched open his car door. He had thought she had come to help, or to see if he was hurt, but instead she had pushed up the sleeve of his jacket, and another woman, coming from behind her, had jabbed a hypodermic needle into his arm.

This was a kidnapping!

But before he could do more than cry out in protest, unconsciousness had swept him into oblivion. He did not know how long the oblivion had lasted. He did remember the half-waking, which came and went. But only now did he begin to remember what had happened; to reason that this had been no accident but a deliberately engineered plot. It was no use asking why; he had to accept the fact, but—

How long had he been here?

And where was he?

For the first time he began to move; that was when he realized that his wrists were tied to the sides of the bed on which he was lying. He moved his fingers, felt the metal on both sides.

It was pitch dark and silent, and whether he liked to admit it or not, he was frightened, for he didn't know what to do.

Gideon reached the canteen to find the Commander of Traffic and a Deputy Commander from Uniform sitting at a table. They gave him a friendly greeting, and he joined them, carrying a bowl of soup and some onion bread on his tray, together with the cutlery he would need.

The Deputy Commander pushed a chair back for him while Rivers, of Traffic, asked straight-faced, "Seen any old jam jars lately, George?"

He laughed. "At the moment, I'm more interested in Elsie."

"Who?" Traffic asked, obviously puzzled.

"Elsie—" began the Deputy Commander. "Oh, I get you! Last night was just the night for the lady," he said.

"I don't know what you're talking about," Traffic said. He was a quiet, thin man with a lantern jaw, and heavily lidded eyes. "Who's Elsie?"

"The Ecology of London Committee," said the Deputy Commander calmly. "Sometimes known as the Enemies of Loving Couples."

"Oh, that bunch." Traffic looked down his nose. "They're a bloody nuisance, always holding meetings at park gates during rush hour. Nearly as bad as the Women's Lib crowd." A promise of a smile showed in his green eyes. "Don't quote me, my wife's all in favor of them! But this Enemies of Loving Couples—" He broke off, stared at the Deputy Commander, and then grinned so widely he seemed to split his long face in two. *"Now* I've got it. E-L-C! Elsie. Well, I'm beggared! I wonder who thought that one up. But what a bunch! They can tack an 'anti' on practically anything worth doing, these days."

"They'll see the light in time," declared the Deputy piously. "By the way, Commander"—he looked at Gideon—"Alec Hobbs was coming to see me this morning. Any idea why he hasn't turned up?"

"No," Gideon said, "but as soon as I'm back in my office, I'm going to find out."

"No one like him at any of the hospital casualty wards," the

61

Information inspector said. "I'm quite sure, sir."

"Well, we've got to find him," Gideon declared. "He made a round of Divisional Headquarters yesterday. Find out the times he visited them and let me know at once."

"Right, sir," promised the inspector. "I know one thing, sir —he went in his own car, that M.G. He told Superintendent Wilberforce at A.B. Division it showed up better at night and on dull days."

"Know the number?" demanded Gideon.

"Yes, sir. KLG—"

"Then get a call out for it at once," Gideon interrupted.

"Right, sir!"

Gideon put back the receiver heavily and sat quite still, acutely aware of the thumping of his heart. He was becoming seriously alarmed for Hobbs. And the measure of his fear told him as nothing else could have done how much the other man had come to mean to him.

Some of his concern was for Penny, of course, but that did not lessen his personal concern. He was trying to convince himself that there was a simple explanation when his inter-office telephone rang. He quickly snatched off the receiver and said, "Gideon."

"Superintendent Bruce here, Commander!" Bruce had never sounded more smug. "I've a report on the soil found adhering to the wash-leather bag. I wonder—"

"What is it?" said Gideon.

"I wonder whether it would be possible for you to spare me *and* my brother a few minutes. I took the specimen to him, in person, and persuaded him to come back with me to make a statement."

Gideon hesitated, then thought with a rush of self-annoyance that he couldn't be rude to a man because he was a brother of Nathaniel Bruce; moreover, the Controller of

62

Parks might be a good man to see. It flashed into his mind that Bruce might have brought his brother over for that very reason, rather than the one he had stated, and he tried to infuse some warmth into his voice as he said, "By all means! Bring him along."

"At once, Commander."

The brother, Sylvester Bruce, could move as fast as the Yard man, for they were at the door in less than sixty seconds, but there the resemblance ended, except perhaps in height. The brother was inches broader, a thick-set man with a weathered face and skin. He wore tweeds, and ankle boots of dark brown leather. His hands were work-roughened, his grip firm.

"And can you identify the soil on the bag?" asked Gideon.

"I can say this," said the other confidently, "it's not from Hyde Park. Most likely from North London—Tottenham, say —or Edmonton. Could be the man who was caught merely picked it up."

"Sylvester, *that* is a police matter," his brother protested.

The other Bruce, probably five or six years the elder, gave a derisory kind of grin.

"Isn't it all a police matter! Don't tell me you didn't bring me to the Commander for more than a bag of diamonds." He shrugged. "Aren't you more interested in all these goings-on in the parks, Commander?"

"Let's say I'm as interested," conceded Gideon, who took to this man as much as he was antagonistic to his brother.

"Fair enough," said Sylvester Bruce. "Well—I've instructed all our park-keepers to cooperate with the police, but I'll admit I've a soft spot for Lady Carradine and her Elsies. The parks are the loveliest part of London. I defy any city in the world to have such displays of flowers. Nor is there anything more beautiful than our flowering shrubs and trees. Don't *you* love the parks, Commander?"

63

Quietly, Gideon said, "Very much. But they aren't only places of beauty, to look at. They *are* places of rest and recreation."

"And procreation?" Sylvester's smile was broad but his voice was sharp.

"Where there have been bushes there have been young lovers ever since I can remember," Gideon said, "and I would hate to see all the bushes destroyed."

"So would I. But if you had the job of cleaning up, you wouldn't be so liberal-minded. Every kind of filth and litter—" Sylvester was beginning to go red in the face. "My God! If I had my way, I'd—"

"Sylvester, please!"

Sylvester turned on his brother, and for a moment Gideon thought that his anger would turn to violence. But he saw a strange thing. Spruce Bruce stood very still, eying his brother with great intentness, until slowly the rage began to die down, and after a while Sylvester gave an explosive little laugh and turned back to Gideon.

"I'm sorry, Commander. I still hope you'll help to clean up the parks."

"You know," Gideon said, "my children played in them, and their children play in them today. Yes. Once we have dealt with the vigilante activities of these ladies, I will do what I can. I'm not sure that the first move shouldn't be with the Parks Department concerned, but I'll have some special kind of surveillance and if my men's reports bear out what you say, I'll send a comprehensive report where it should do some good."

After a pause, Spruce Bruce said, "You are very good, Commander."

"*Very* good," echoed his brother. "I didn't think you would live up to Nat's high opinion of you, but you do."

"Now if you'll live up to his opinion of you and help us with these ladies," Gideon said, and all three laughed; it was one of the best moments of Gideon's day.

When the brothers had gone, he began to wonder whether the situation was as bad as the older Bruce made out.

8

The Car

THAT MORNING, the story of Gideon and his jam jar had spread through the Yard, as it were, on wings.

But just as a laugh or a joke could travel quickly, so also could alarm.

Now the alarm was about Hobbs.

A dozen—perhaps two dozen—policemen knew what car Hobbs drove for his own pleasure, and its number. Once the description was out in a priority message to all divisions and subdivisional stations, another word went with it.

Hobbs's car had been stolen!

At first, that was a bigger joke than Gideon's jam jar, but it was short-lived. The fair-haired constable in Information was laughing at the enormity of the joke—who would have the nerve to steal the Deputy Commander's car, and wouldn't Hobbs's face be red?—when the inspector to whom Gideon had talked said roughly, "This isn't funny. The D.C. was in it when it was last seen."

"My God!"

"Don't spread that around, but just concentrate on stolen cars."

"Don't spread that around" was like telling the wind not to blow. From lips to lips the words went, "Do you know what —*Hobbs* is missing!"

"Hobbs?"

"The D.C."

"You can't be serious."

"It's a fact—*Hobbs* is missing."

"Alec *Hobbs?*"

"Yes."

"But I saw him only yesterday afternoon."

"I saw him—"

"No one's seen him today."

"Who did see him last?"

"He was at Hampstead, with me," a red-faced superintendent at the K.L. Division said. "Left about half past four. I'll check. . . . It was a quarter past four."

"The car was in the car park behind N.W. Headquarters."

"*I* saw him out," a constable boasted. "It was getting very thick by then; I asked him if he was sure he could make it. He said he was."

"Which way did he go?"

"He went towards the Pond, could have gone anywhere from there."

"Anyone thought of dragging the Pond at Hampstead Heath?" a wag asked.

"That's *not* funny."

The red-faced man at K.L. was given these reports, and took the almost unprecedented step of talking to all the men in his division who had been on duty the previous afternoon; it was comparatively easy because the same shift was being worked now and there were few changes. His name was Jack Sharp; he had a decisive, rather clipped voice.

"I want you to discuss this with your colleagues. I want *any* information you can give me about the car, already described to you, and Mr. Hobbs. And I want reports of anything at all unusual noticed in the area."

But the fog had blinkered both sight and sound. Men who had seen a white M.G. had not seen the driver closely, nor had it been possible to note the number. All the reports were negative until Sharp called Gideon, in the middle of the afternoon.

"About Mr. Hobbs's car, Commander—"

"Have you traced it?" Gideon demanded.

"No, sir, but it was parked here until four-fifteen, and I've some reports of a similar car going along— Do you know Hampstead?"

"Well enough."

"It was seen near Ken Wood, that is the last official report," Sharp went on. "Do you know if there were any distinguishing marks on the tires?"

"No." Gideon looked at a report which had come up from Information. "It has Dunlops on the front and one rear wheel, Michelin on the other—near-side—front wheel. Why?"

"It was very damp yesterday and there was rain at the weekend—and there are a lot of private dirt roads and drives —good area for tire prints. I thought I'd send out word."

"Do that," Gideon urged, and rang off. He felt more anxious than ever.

About the time that Superintendent Sharp was talking to Gideon, one of the oldest men on the divisional staff was standing at a corner where he had stood on the previous day, although then it had been half an hour later. He was rather stout, and it was a long time since he had moved very fast, longer since he had known the slightest ambition. He was not an unhappy man, he lived comfortably in a house in Kensal Green, his wife worked in the canteen of a small factory, all their children were away from home.

This man, Police Constable Best, had probably the least distinguished career of anyone in the Force; yet he had a high level of competence, and training had taught him to use his memory. Ever since the call for the Deputy Commander's M.G. had gone out, he had tried to recall where he had seen a similar car yesterday.

Now he remembered.

He was at the corner of Hampstead Lane and one of the innumerable private roads that branched from it. On this corner was a large Victorian house with a "FOR SALE" notice on a board in the front garden. He passed it twice a day on his rounds, keeping a lookout for young vandals who might hurl stones at the windows, or any sign that hippies had taken possession.

He had seen the car just here.

He could not honestly say that he had recognized the driver, but he had certainly noticed his dark hair and the fact that he was rather older than most drivers of sports cars.

It had disappeared.

Ah! He had another gradual return of memory; a few seconds, perhaps half a minute after seeing it, he had heard a crash. Not a loud one, and somewhere behind him. On a clear day, P.C. Best might have been able to turn round and see what had happened. As it was, he had paused and pondered, then decided to go and investigate, but as he had started off an elderly woman with a Yorkshire terrier on a leash came out of the fog. If there was one animal Best liked above all others, it was a dog, and he had a special liking for small ones.

He approached the woman and the dog with the encouraging clicks of the tongue dog lovers commonly suppose dogs like. This one did not appear to do so, but Constable Best remained undaunted. Its elderly owner, swift to take advantage of Best's interest, volunteered the information that she lived in Ebury Court and had temporarily lost her sense of direction. Constable Best saw her safely home and, with a last loving glance at the Yorkshire terrier, made his way back to the spot where he thought the crash had been. There was a litter of broken headlamp glass near the curb, so he hadn't been wrong; but there could have been no real harm done, and it had not seemed worth reporting when he went off duty.

But if it had been the wanted car—

"I'd better report it now," he told himself, "just in case." He called the station.

"Stay there," he was told promptly. "This one's urgent."

P.C. Best, mourning his tardiness of last night, searched for tire marks and found them. Five minutes later, a police car pulled up. The two occupants, one a C.I.D. man, joined him.

"There's a Michelin print here," the C.I.D. man said.

"And here. It looks as if it did a U-turn."

"Bloody silly thing to do."

"Well, look." The first man pointed to tire marks that were quite unmistakable. "That car stopped on the collision, and then did a U-turn. Better trace it back. Will you pick up as much of that glass as you can?" he added to Best.

Methodically, Best began to collect the pieces of shattered glass, while the plainclothesman and the driver of the police car went slowly along, keeping to the middle of the road. Now and again tire prints showed, but there was no certainty they were Michelin. They came to the Victorian house with the sale board.

"Stop a moment," the C.I.D. man said. "Let's have a look in that driveway." Muddy sand had gathered not only at one side but right across the drive in places, and there was no doubt of the Michelin tire print.

Hot on the scent, the men followed the drive to the side of the house, where all prints disappeared on gravel on which grass and weeds were growing. Straight ahead, perhaps fifty yards from the back of the house, was a brick garage, the wooden doors secured with a bar and locked with a hasp and padlock.

"That hasp's rusty," one of the men remarked. "The padlock might have been bought yesterday. Any windows?"

They made a quick round of the garage; there was a window on each side, but both were boarded up.

"Let's get those doors open," the C.I.D. man urged.

The driver, a stocky man with powerful shoulders, attacked the doors with professional zest. At the third attack the hasp broke, and the doors sagged open.

Both men started forward, their eyes fixed on the back of a small white car bearing the number KLG–231X.

"That's it!" cried the C.I.D. man. "That's the car! It—"

He broke off, and gulped.

The other said uneasily, "Well, we've found the car. Have we found the D.C.?"

For slumping forward over the wheel was the body of a man.

They approached slowly, one on each side. The body was so still it might have been a dummy. It was the C.I.D. man who spoke next, with a ring of relief in his voice.

"Whoever it is, it isn't Hobbs. He's dark and this chap's hair—" His voice quivered into silence.

"That's not hair," the police driver said bluntly, "that's blood."

Both of them stood still, as still as the man slumped over the wheel of Hobbs's car. He had been battered to death.

Only a mile or so away, the young man named Lennie Sappo nursed his secret. It worried him. He kept seeing images of the face of the man being forced into that house at Cricklewood. Kept hearing the other man threatening to kill him. He hadn't waited to see more for fear of being caught.

Well, it wasn't *his* business. Ever since he could remember, his parents had told him, "Don't stick your nose in anybody else's affair. Just keep your mouth shut and you'll be all right."

But Lennie Sappo wished there were one person, just one, he could talk to.

9

The Missing Car

GIDEON PICKED UP the telephone at twenty to five, said "Gideon," and wondered what triviality this would be; to him everything but the search for Hobbs had now become trivial. The instant that the caller began to speak, he knew that it was Sharp, of Hampstead, in K.L., and his whole body went tense.

"We've found Hobbs's car," Sharp said. "But not Hobbs."

"Where?"

"In the garage of an empty house," Sharp replied. There was a curious hesitation about the way he spoke; it screamed a warning, for normally Sharp was the most incisive of men. "Commander—" He broke off, but Gideon had the sense to wait. "There was—is—a dead man at the wheel."

Gideon heard and yet did not fully take it in. A dead man at the wheel of Hobbs's car in a deserted garage. Sharp said nothing, and quickly Gideon regained control of himself.

"How did he die?"

"It looks like murder."

"Do we know him?"

"No one who's seen him has recognized him, but we've taken fingerprints. They're on the way to Records now."

"I'll come over," Gideon said decisively. "I'd like to have a word with the man who found the car—tell me about it on the radio as I come. I'll need a word with the Commissioner, then I'll be on the way. Press on the scene yet?"

"No—the discovery wasn't made until twenty minutes ago." That was Sharp's way of making sure Gideon knew how quickly he'd been informed.

"Good work," Gideon said.

He rang off and immediately dialed Fingerprints, where one of the older men at the Yard, Nicholson, was still in charge.

"Some fingerprints are on the way from Mr. Sharp at Hampstead," Gideon said. "They could not be more urgent. Send someone to Records with them as soon as you've got good specimens. Let me know, send a copy of a report to the Commissioner's office, and telephone Mr. Sharp."

"Yes, sir!"

Gideon grunted, and rang off; hesitated, and then dialed the number of the Commissioner, Sir Reginald Scott-Marle. He had known the Chief of the Metropolitan Force for many years and was on good terms with him—as good as, if not better than, anyone at the Yard. Yet when it came to calling him about some new situation Gideon always felt a moment's uncertainty, almost diffidence.

The bell rang six times and then Scott-Marle's brisk, clear voice came over the wire. "This is the Commissioner."

"Gideon, sir," Gideon said.

"George," said the Commissioner, "what is this rumor I hear about Hobbs being missing?"

Of course, Gideon thought, such a rumor was bound to reach him; it would have been wiser to tell him at the start.

"It's more than a rumor now, sir, I'm afraid. His car has been found, and in it the body of a murdered man."

"Good God!"

"I'm just on my way to Hampstead," Gideon said. "How late will you be in the office, sir?"

"Call me, and if I'm not here, call me at home," Scott-Marle ordered.

"I'll do that, sir," Gideon said.

He replaced the receiver and strode out of his office, chin thrust forward in an aggressive tilt. He turned in to a men's room, for which only a favored few had a key, as a small man with a very lined face was coming out. This was Chief Detective Superintendent Piluski, busy on an investigation concerning immigration, whom Gideon must soon see.

"Any word from Mr. Hobbs, sir?" Piluski asked.

"Nasty rumors," Gideon said. "I'm going to see what I can make of them now."

Soon he was in the back of a big and comfortable limousine, with a peak-capped driver at the wheel. The traffic was very thick; everyone seemed to be on the move early in an attempt to beat any return of the fog. But his driver knew the short cuts and Gideon was able to talk, via Information, to Sharp at Hampstead. This time Sharp was quite himself, recovered from the shock he had received earlier.

"No more news, sir," he reported. "But I've talked to one of our constables who was on beat duty yesterday. He remembers one or two things that may be helpful."

"Why didn't we know about it yesterday?"

"There was nothing to know," Sharp replied. "It wasn't until the call for the car went out that our chap—" He told the story in some detail, obviously anxious that the constable, Best, should get full credit. "Best is to retire at the end of the year, sir," he added.

Gideon said, "Tell me that bit about the woman who got lost with her dog."

"Could easily happen to anyone last night," Sharp replied, and repeated what Best had told him.

Gideon rubbed the lobe of his left ear, and then asked slowly, "A Yorkshire terrier, you say?"

"That's right."

"Have you checked at this block of flats, Ebury Court, to see if such a woman and dog live there?"

There was a startled pause, which answered Gideon before Sharp actually replied, "No, I haven't."

"Better make sure she exists," Gideon said.

"I'll know within half an hour," Sharp promised, in a voice that betrayed his anger with himself. "Anything else now, Commander?"

"Press still unaware of what's happened?"

"I had a call from the *Daily Echo* to ask whether it was true we'd found a dead man in an unused garage," Sharp replied, "but the man didn't link it with Mr. Hobbs."

"Hold them off as long as you can," urged Gideon.

He looked out onto the crowded pavements, seeing a girl of Penny's coloring and build, which brought his daughter sharply to his mind. What would she do? How could he tell her what had happened? In a surprisingly short time the car reached Swiss Cottage, but there the traffic was really thick, and when they weren't standing still they were crawling. No news came over the radio-telephone, and Gideon had time to let everything that had happened pass through his mind; and he even began to speculate.

Was Hobbs hurt?

Had he been taken away against his will? *Kidnapped?* The very word was anathema where a policeman was concerned, but it recurred again and again. It was unthinkable, yet he was thinking about it.

Why should the word occur to him? Why not wonder whether Hobbs was alive?

Because, if whoever'd stolen his car had wanted to kill him, presumably they could have done so as readily as they had killed the man found slumped over the wheel.

At last the car turned in to the street where the Divisional Headquarters were, and as it slowed down Gideon saw one policeman duck indoors, while another came forward, obviously prepared to receive Gideon. The first man was alerting Sharp and the whole station, of course.

He was right about that, for Sharp was in the hall to meet him.

Before Sharp had finished shaking hands, he spoke: "Word came through from Records. Those prints aren't known."

"Pity," Gideon gloomed.

"Nor is a little old lady with a Yorkshire terrier known at Ebury Court," Sharp said ruefully. "It so happens that it's one of the few apartment buildings around here where they won't allow pets. I've got P.C. Best busy trying to recall every last detail of her face," he added. "Would you like to see him before we go round to the Towers house?"

"What do you advise?"

"He's a bit jumpy," Sharp replied. "Nearly thirty years with the Force and this is the first time he's run into anything like this. I think he'll bear being left on his own for a bit."

"Then let's leave him," Gideon agreed readily. "I'd like to see the car, and the body."

"We'll go in my car—it's parked at the back, and we needn't go upstairs to my office until later," Sharp declared. "My God! I'm mad at myself for not thinking that woman could have been there to stop Best from going to see what was happening." When Gideon didn't answer him, and they stepped out into a well-lit car park behind the police station, he went on: "If that's what she was there for, it's a pretty well-organized job." He paused to give Gideon another chance to speak, but Gideon preferred to listen. "And what's a little old woman doing in a case where a man's head was smashed in? I'll vow one thing, Commander. Whoever struck the blows had the strength of an ox. Only a young and very fit woman could have used such force."

"Or a man," Gideon said.

"Oh, of course—or a man," Sharp agreed with alacrity. "Or a man."

Gideon looked hard at the face of the victim.

It was scarcely marked; the blows had been struck from behind, and death must have been almost instantaneous. The body had not been moved, except to raise the head for identification purposes, and to enable photographers to take pictures fullface. The last pictures were being taken as Gideon went into the big cold garage.

A plastic sheet had been spread over the back of the car, and two men were examining the bucket seats. They were being meticulously careful, but one thing was apparent at a glance.

"No blood splashes," Gideon remarked.

"So he wasn't killed here," stated Sharp.

"Doesn't look like it, sir," said one of the men cheerfully.

"Any blood anywhere?" asked Gideon.

"Only the head and neck, the shoulders and a few spots on the shirt, as far as we can judge," the man replied.

"Police surgeon been here yet?"

"Yes, sir—and he's coming back."

Gideon nodded, and looked about the garage. It had a

cement floor, cracked in places where weeds struggled to grow. In one corner was what looked like a bed of soil filled with roots: probably dahlias, Gideon thought. The small windows had been boarded up for years; the nails fastening the boards to the window frames were rusty and bent.

A tall, schoolboyish-looking man came hurrying in, and out of the corner of his mouth Sharp said, "Peel, the police surgeon."

"Sorry," he said. "I was in the house."

"Is the water laid on there?" asked Gideon.

"No, sir. The place looks as if it's been empty for years."

"Two years," Sharp intervened.

"What opinion do you have about the cause of death?" Gideon asked Peel.

"The man died from wounds inflicted by a flat, blunt instrument," Peel stated without the slightest hesitation. "An autopsy might reveal poison but, judging from appearances, the blows were the cause of death."

"Estimated time?" asked Gideon.

"Between six and eight or nine o'clock, last night," the young police surgeon answered. "*Rigor* was well in when I first saw him half an hour ago. He wasn't killed here, that's certain. Blood would have spattered. I'd say it had coagulated good and hard before he was put in here."

"Why?" Gideon was intrigued and impressed; and had a feeling that Sharp was mildly amused.

"The depth of the coagulation helped to indicate the time of death," the police surgeon said, "and I'd say he was stiff when he was put in that seat. There's some evidence of force to bend the knees and hips. Also"—the man looked up at a cross strut which helped to support the roof—"his head was banged against that and some dried blood came off, but there was no evidence of fresh bleeding. I'd say he was carried into

79

the garage, held upright until he was placed in the front seat, and his head was banged as he was placed in position. Mind you, sir"—Peel gave a sudden flashing smile—"this isn't conclusive, but I don't think I'm far wrong."

"I'll take your word for it," Gideon said briefly. "He was brought here about the time the fog was at its worst, then?"

"It certainly looks like it," agreed the police surgeon.

"That doesn't give us much chance of finding any witnesses," Sharp remarked. "But I'd better get cracking. House to house?" he asked.

"Yes," agreed Gideon. "House to house. (a) Did anyone see the M.G.? (b) Did anyone see or hear the accident? (c) Did anyone see any other vehicle just before or just after the accident—say, between four o'clock and five?" Gideon paused only for a moment before going on with the same positiveness. "Did anyone see this old lady and her Yorkshire terrier? That's (d), and (e) Who in this part of the world has a Yorkshire? Any woman's footprints in the road?" he added.

"We're rechecking," Sharp told him. "Are you going to stay here for a bit, sir?"

"Yes," Gideon answered. "Come back when you've put everything in hand, will you?" He walked with the local Superintendent to the doors of the garage.

It was now pitch dark.

A street lamp was shining, not far away. Several policemen had their torches on and one car was illuminating the drive of the house with its headlights. Gideon went on with Sharp, silent now: there was a limit to how far he should go in telling a senior officer what to do. Sharp got into his car and was driven off, and Gideon turned back.

A man who had been standing just inside the grounds of the house moved toward him, and said in a well-controlled, low-pitched voice, "It must be a very significant case to bring you out in person, Commander. Is it true that Alec Hobbs is missing?"

On the instant of seeing him, Gideon knew who this was: one of Fleet Street's most astute and knowledgeable newspapermen—Jefferson Jackson, of the *Echo*.

Quite suddenly Gideon found himself in the midst of a crisis of decision.

10

Crisis

THERE WAS NO POINT at all in being evasive or in telling this man half-truths. The one thing that might gain time was a statement conditional upon its being off the record for a specified time. But Gideon was not yet sure whether he wanted it to be off the record. This might well be a case in which the newspapers, as well as radio and television, would help much more than hinder. He could be formal, of course, and promise a statement later, but that would not make much difference to Jefferson Jackson, who must have missed the evening edition of his companion paper, anyhow.

The newspaperman waited patiently.

"I don't want to admit it, but yes," Gideon answered at last. "If he doesn't turn up soon, I shall ask you chaps to meet me at the Yard later, and I shall ask radio and television channels to help."

"So it's as bad as that," Jefferson Jackson said, a little taken aback by Gideon's straightforward admission of the facts. *"Is* that his M.G.?"

"Yes."

"*Is* there a body in it?"

Gideon said, "Yes, of an unknown man apparently killed by blows on the head, by means of the usual blunt instrument. And no, I don't know what it's about—yet," he added. Then he asked, "Do you?"

"No," Jackson answered briskly. "Commander—*can* this mean that the Deputy Commander C.I.D. has been kidnapped?"

"Possibly."

"Could it conceivably mean that *he* killed the dead man?"

"To me, such a supposition is quite inconceivable."

"But it might not be to others." There was sharpness in Jackson's voice; his face had taken on the look of a ferret about to attack.

"I can't help what idiot ideas other people might get," Gideon said, with obvious impatience. "I hope *you*'ll have enough sense to know it's not possible."

"Not even in the line of duty?"

"Not without reporting it immediately—and in any case, not in this way," Gideon said flatly. "There will be an official statement later tonight. Meanwhile you're at liberty to use anything I've said." He shifted his position, as if in dismissal.

"Commander," Jackson said quietly, "is Elsie involved?"

Gideon hesitated. Jackson couldn't know that Elsie was new to Gideon. After a moment, he said, "What do you know about Elsie?"

"The Ecology of London Committee," Jackson answered. "Or—"

"The Enemies of Loving Couples," Gideon said dryly.

"Hobbs was working on that."

"Did he tell you so?"

"I don't always have to be told," the *Echo* man said.

83

"You might be wise to have your guesses confirmed," Gideon advised, forcing a lighter note into his voice. "I don't particularly want E.L.C. to be mentioned yet."

"That's a pity," said Jackson.

"Why?"

"I propose to do a feature article about it for tomorrow. In fact, the feature is done, all but the finishing touches. I've reason to believe your deputy in the C.I.D. was investigating the activities of E.L.C., and I've no reason to withhold the fact."

"You must please yourself," Gideon said.

"*Or* the fact that a lifelong friend of Alec Hobbs, a very attractive young woman named Hilda Jessop, is also involved in some way or other?" Jackson asked, in a very soft voice. "That's the kind of topic that our readers delight in, Commander. And they are always fascinated by the fact that your youngest daughter and the Deputy Commander are engaged."

It was now glaringly obvious to Gideon that Jackson was deliberately goading him; that last remark could have no other interpretation. Could there be any reason beyond the fact that Jackson hoped that by making Gideon lose his temper he would learn more? Gideon looked down on him without expression, and then turned away. There were questions he would like to ask this man, about Elsie and what he knew of Hobbs's interest in it, and what part Hilda Jessop was playing, but to ask questions now would be to betray his ignorance; he didn't want to do that.

There wasn't much more he could do here, but it was difficult to leave before Sharp returned. He *could* try to get the Commissioner on the radio-telephone of one of the police cars; he decided to, and swung round.

Jackson, apparently satisfied, was driving off in a Morris

1100, vivid scarlet in the street lamp. Before he squeezed into the police car, next to the driver, Gideon took a long look at the newspaperman's car as it moved away.

He had no doubt what to do next. He made a thorough search of Hobbs's office, but found no notes or reports that had not already been received officially. He then went on to Hobbs's flat, taking a detective sergeant with him. Absolutely nothing was found here, except a thank-you note from Hilda for taking her to dinner. If Hobbs knew more than he had put in his reports, it seemed that he kept it all in his head.

What he did not know was that Hobbs had carried a briefcase with him.

Gideon came back to the Yard, and immediately went to see Scott-Marle.

As Gideon was talking to Scott-Marle, Alec Hobbs was lying on his back on what he now knew was a camp bed in a small, barely furnished room; a little light came in at the door to reveal a chair and a table.

He still had no idea what the time was; although his watch was on his wrist, it wasn't ticking. He reasoned that he had been here for at least twenty-four hours; his watch was an automatic winder that never stopped provided he kept the normal use of his left arm.

He had tested the tightness of the bonds at his wrists, and doubted whether there was any chance to free himself. Each wrist appeared to be fastened separately to the side of the bed.

There were quivers of cramp in his right leg, and he was acutely aware of the need for the bathroom.

Inside the house—if it was a house—there was no sound, except occasionally a creak in wall or ceiling, window or door.

He must have been kidnapped twenty-four hours ago, then;

and drugged so that he had been unconscious for most of that time.

He began to ask himself why; began to use his mind, which in itself told him he was back to full consciousness. The edge of fear had gone, but there was an ache of apprehension that spread from his chest throughout his whole body.

There must be a reason: a very significant one. Even in these days of hijacking airplanes and kidnapping politicians and diplomats, there had to be a reason, and usually whoever committed the crime was desperate. It was just possible that he had been taken in mistake for someone else, but to dwell on that possibility would be useless. Much better to believe that he, Alec Vavasour Hobbs, had been kidnapped because he was a senior official of the police.

Was it because of a case he was working on?

Or was it for a general reason: that any senior policeman or, for that matter, any civil servant would have done just as well?

He tried to ease his leg but only succeeded in making the cramp worse. He gritted his teeth against the pain as the muscles of his leg became like iron; he found himself gasping and knew that sweat was on his forehead and his lips.

Slowly the cramp eased, and its final cessation brought an enormous relief.

Soon afterward, he heard a sound.

He lay almost without breathing, praying for it to be repeated; and yes, there was the unmistakable closing of a door, and he thought it was beneath him. Now he began to breathe faster but in shallow breaths, to make sure he heard every movement. There were footsteps on a passage; footsteps on stairs. Man's or woman's? Small man's, he thought, or a woman with a very firm tread. They drew nearer, he had no doubt at all. The wall and the floor of this room creaked; it was a gimcrack place. *She was coming nearer and nearer.* He no longer doubted it was a woman.

She was on the other side of the wall where he was lying. She was at the door.

My God, if she didn't stop—

She stopped, and for what seemed an age there was no sound at all; then he heard a click of metal, and thought, She's taking out keys. Yes, yes, she was: he heard metal scratch on metal, followed by a sharp click of the lock going back. Immediately the door opened and light flooded in, throwing a black shadow on the wall that he could just see. He turned his head to stare, but because the light was behind her he could make out only the shape of her head, the hair piled up in a bun, and square, tailored shoulders.

She drew nearer and, without a word, bent over him and put both hands behind his neck; she was loosening the gag. As it loosened and the blood flowed back to his lips, he was aware of agonizing pain.

Next, she unfastened one of his wrists, then the other.

He tried to lift his arms, but there was no strength in them.

Carefully she eased him off the bed onto his feet. He staggered and, but for her outthrust arm, would have fallen. The uncanny thing was that she had not yet uttered a word; and still without a word, she supported him and, making him put his weight on his legs, headed out of the room along a passage to an open door—the door of a bathroom.

Then she spoke.

"If you want to live," she said, "you won't try to get away."

"Why—" he croaked, and then: "Who—"

But she turned from him, back to the room from which she had freed him, while he lurched into the bathroom, hardly able to place one foot before the other. This wouldn't last; ten or fifteen minutes should see the worst of the weakness over, but—

"If you want to live," she had said, "you won't try to get away."

He had no doubt at all that she meant it.

The bathroom window had been bricked up, a long time— months or years—ago. There was only a small ventilation hole with a fan. It was almost as if this place had been used as a prison before. He stayed long enough to be able to flex the muscles of his legs and arms; to wash, drying himself on paper towels that rasped over his stubble. If he had had any doubt before, he knew now that he had been kidnapped for at least twenty-four hours.

There was nothing in the room he could use as a weapon.

In any case, was this the time to attempt to escape? Wasn't it the time to wait, and try to find out why all this had happened?

Nevertheless he felt an overwhelming temptation to try to get away; to put this nightmare behind him. To get word to Penny and reassure her, to tell Gideon there was no need to worry. The woman here could simply have tried to scare him, and if she was alone in the house he might have a good chance. He went out of the bathroom and looked along the passage to the head of the stairs. The door of his "cell" was open, but there were no sounds and the woman was out of sight. He crept to the head of the stairs. This must be a trick, of course; a ruse to find out whether he would attempt to get away.

He stared down the stairs, and a man's voice said, "Don't try it, mate."

Hobbs started, the voice was so unexpected. It came from the narrow passage at the side of the stairs, from a man who was leaning against the wall and grinning up at him.

In the man's right hand was a revolver.

Hobbs moistened his lips, and said, "You know you'll get into serious trouble for this, don't you?" His voice was stronger than he had expected; there was even some authority in it.

"Been in trouble all me life, copper," the man replied. "Wouldn't feel natural if I wasn't. Be a good boy, now, and go back to your bedroom. Clara will bring you something to eat in a few minutes, and she might even let you have a radio. You can never tell with Clara. But—" He moved to the foot of the stairs, changing the gun from one hand to the other. "Lemme give you a word of warning about her. Don't try any tricks. She's as strong as any man and she knows the tender spots. She's got a very cruel streak, Clara has, so don't upset her."

The impulse to jump—to close with the man, to get the gun from him—was almost irresistible. Hobbs stood at the top of the stairs gritting his teeth, while the man grinned up at him. As they stood, footsteps came clear and unmistakable. Clara appeared, carrying a laden tray.

"Get out of my way, you clod," she said to the man, and he obeyed. Hobbs turned and went back into his room. She followed him, putting the tray on the table. There was a plastic knife and fork, a bowl of what might be soup, two crusty hunks of bread, a slab of butter, and a piece of cheese.

"Any trouble from you and back you go to that bed," she declared. She had a square face with a thin mouth, but was not ill-looking and her eyes were an attractive brown. She took a small transistor radio from a pocket of her jacket and placed it next to the tray.

Then she went out, locking the door behind her.

It was senseless to sulk, to delay eating. Hobbs pulled up the only chair in the room, sat down, and took the lid off the bowl. The steam and the aroma which arose took him completely by surprise. This was a stew, with dumplings, chunks of meat, and vegetables; and he knew before he tasted it that it was going to be full of flavor.

"Well, they're not going to starve me," he said aloud. "Or keep me isolated."

He switched on the radio, then settled down to eat.

While he ate, his mind clicked into the right channels. If this kidnapping was because of a case he was involved in, then there were only three possible cases.

The jewel robberies were an obvious first, but Bruce knew more than he did about them. Yet he did know a great deal, and if his kidnappers wanted to find out what the police were doing about them, he was a better man to question than Bruce. Did they—could anybody—seriously believe that he would talk? They might think he would under pressure; there was literally no telling what methods of persuasion they would use. In all, nearly half a million pounds' worth of jewels had been stolen, and the thieves would probably take great risks and go to unprecedented lengths to get away with it.

The Hale & Commyns case was another possibility, but less likely; the company was obviously fraudulent and knew that the truth would be found out before long. The men involved might flee the country, but—no, he didn't see that they would take this kind of action.

It couldn't—it *couldn't* be the E.L.C. affair, could it?

He felt a stab of uneasiness. Some of its members were fanatics, and there was no way of being sure that they wouldn't break the law if they thought it would serve their purpose. He had hoped only this morning to learn more about them from Hilda, but—

He drew in a sharp breath as a possibility flashed into his mind.

Was it conceivable that he had been kidnapped to prevent

him from seeing her and so learn some particular clue she had come upon?

Oh, nonsense!

He finished eating, and pushed the chair back, disgruntled not only with the situation but with the limited range of his thinking. He stared at the radio—wasn't it ever going to broadcast the news?

There was a break in the music, six pips sounded the time signal, followed by the announcer saying, in his brisk way, "This is Radio Four of the British Broadcasting Service with the nine-o'clock news. Before the news, a statement is to be made by Commander George Gideon, Chief of the Criminal Investigation Department at Scotland Yard, who has a request to make to all members of the general public, particularly those who were in or near Hampstead yesterday afternoon between four o'clock and five. This statement will be broadcast on all radio and all television channels. Please stand by." There was another pause before Gideon's voice sounded, deep and clear.

Hobbs no longer had any doubt why he had been allowed a radio.

"If there was just *someone* I could talk to," Lennie Sappo was saying to himself. He was bothered, even though this was his lucky night; he was crowded in with a dozen others, watching television in a radio and repair shop. If he could, he would stay until the last program; he didn't mind what it was.

11

The Appeal

THE TELEVISION LIGHTS burned dazzling bright. The studio where Gideon sat was unbearably hot. There were three microphones in front of him, and he was alone except for the camera crew. He knew that a group of technicians were in another room, working their mighty miracles and sending pictures and sound out to millions of listeners and viewers. But he had been before television cameras often and wasn't nervous, even though he was more anxious than he could remember ever having been.

"It is not often that the Metropolitan Police asks the British Broadcasting Corporation and the Independent Television Authority for this privilege," he began. "Because it is not often that a situation of such gravity arises. The law—the police are often challenged by criminals, and you all know that there is a constant state of war between us." He paused long enough for the significance of what he said to sink in, and then went on: "The Home Secretary and the Commissioner of

Police both agree that a situation has arisen which could become extremely dangerous; could lead to a more dangerous open challenge to authority by some criminals than this country has ever known. And it is simply this: my deputy, Deputy Commander Hobbs, has been abducted. It is not yet known why, but it is known that at least one murder has been committed in connection with the abduction. It is also beyond all reasonable doubt that this is an effort to force the authorities to take a certain course of action, by pressure of their anxiety for the safety of a very fine police officer."

Gideon paused again. . . .

Hobbs sat, unmoving.

Penelope, during the interval of the concert her orchestra was giving in Liverpool, watched tensely, her hands clenched.

Kate Gideon, alone in the middle room of the house in Harrington Street, heard her husband's words; her face was pale.

Hilda Jessop, also alone, sat in an expensive flat in Knightsbridge watching this man, with his strong face and deep, penetrating voice, and seeing what she had glimpsed at his office: a combination of power, of ruthlessness, and authority. What this man had to do, he would do.

The mass of ordinary people, unknown, unknowing, were yet drawn by the compulsive power of the speaker, held as if by some great star; gripped as much by how he said what he had to say as by the burden of his message.

A little woman in a small apartment in Hampstead sat watching; on her lap a Yorkshire terrier lay asleep.

All the members, men and women, of the Ecology of London Committee watched.

Many park-keepers watched, not knowing how they might be affected.

Alfie, at the garage in New King's Road, sat holding his breath as he watched his hero.

P.C. Arthur Simpson and P.C. Best watched intently.

Every criminal who was not out on a job watched Gideon's face and listened to the voice of a man who was at once their archenemy and a man whom they all respected, even those with cause to hate him.

It seemed, indeed, as if all Britain saw and heard, which was what Gideon wanted above all.

He did not realize it, but the intensity of his feeling was such that all who saw and heard were aware of it; and were gripped by a sense of the danger to society which could grow out of the abduction of a policeman.

"It must be understood by everyone concerned that we shall not yield to pressure; that we are the upholders of the law, and that it is the law which upholds the rights of the people." Gideon paused, straightened his great shoulders, and continued: "I want to ask everyone who might conceivably know anything which could help us to find Mr. Hobbs to telephone the nearest police station or the nearest newspaper office *at once.* There are some who may, knowingly or unknowingly, have seen or heard something of vital importance that night at the corner of Hampstead Lane and Pleasance Street, when the fog was at its thickest. . . ."

A photograph of the corner appeared behind him and gradually filled the screen.

"Here is the car. . . ."

A picture of the white M.G. showed next and was held for a few seconds, before gradually fading and being superseded by a photograph of Alec Hobbs. It was a good studio portrait, taken for Penny; in his dark-haired, even-featured way, Hobbs was very handsome.

It was almost as if millions drew in their breath at sight of him.

"The car, or the man, might have been seen in many parts of London yesterday," Gideon went on. "But we are interested *only* in the time between four and five o'clock, because we are almost sure that soon after five o'clock the car was in this garage."

A picture of the house known as The Towers was shown, with the "FOR SALE" notice, and shifted slowly to the open doors of the garage. Slowly, slowly, the camera seemed to draw the car toward it; lights were now on in the garage, focusing on the car, the number plate, the plastic sheet.

"With a dead man, a murdered man, sitting where Mr. Hobbs had been a very short time before," Gideon told his audience, and again it was as if the millions drew in a short, sharp breath of horror.

The head and shoulders of the dead man showed for an agonizing moment; then Gideon appeared again, as solid as if he would never change. He leaned forward to give his point due emphasis.

"There may be people among you who saw Alec Hobbs after the attack. You may have seen him prisoner in another car; or entering or leaving a car or a house. If you have any reason to think you did, tell the police or the press *at once.* The slightest clue could give us the vital information we need.

"And there are almost certainly among you some who took part in the abduction. The little old lady with the Yorkshire terrier, for instance . . ."

A few miles away, the little old lady clutched her dog so tightly that he woke with a start.

"There are the individuals who actually carried out this abduction," Gideon went on. "There are those who ordered it. There are the leaders and those who work for the leaders. I promise any and every one of you who were involved in the crime the utmost consideration if you will telephone me—or any police station—or any newspaper office—telling where to find Alec Hobbs. Or where we might find him. Or where we will find anyone who can give us the information we need.

"This is not simply a matter of catching a criminal.

"It is a matter of defending and protecting the whole fabric of our society."

The camera held him for a moment—for a much longer period than it usually held its subject—but gradually the picture faded, and the voice died away.

It did not die in Hobbs's ears. It echoed and re-echoed, and when he closed his eyes he could see Gideon as clearly as the millions had seen him. He heard the footsteps on the stairs, became aware of the sound of the key turning in the lock, and of the door opening.

The woman Clara said, "He must be crazy, to think we'd grass."

Hobbs looked at her.

"And you'd better hope he changes his mind," Clara went on aggressively. *"You* are going to be part of a deal, Alec Hobbs. No deal, no Alec Hobbs—just a body." She took the tray and backed toward the door, showing some sign of nervousness for the first time. "And I don't mean maybe."

She backed out as Hobbs gripped the sides of the table.

Before he could move, even before he had decided whether to move, the man with the gun appeared in the doorway.

He gave a grin of derision, then pulled the door to; a moment later the key turned in the lock.

Almost before Gideon had finished talking, the telephone calls began to come in with reports of Hobbs, of white M.G.s, of old ladies with Yorkshire terriers being seen in a dozen, a hundred parts of London at the same time. The police checked every report thoroughly, but there were not enough men to keep on top of the job, even when hundreds were drafted in from neighboring divisions. The newspapers were printing Gideon's broadcast verbatim, emphasizing the fight between crime and society, the fact that no principles could be sacrificed for any individual policeman.

Even old convicts telephoned, some with mock condolence but many with genuine good will.

Meanwhile every policeman on duty in the London area was on the lookout for an elderly woman with a Yorkshire terrier. She would probably be frightened. She might, Gideon knew, be so frightened that she would kill and bury the dog.

There was one other possibility that preyed on Gideon's mind.

She herself might be killed to make sure she could not talk.

Her name was Geraldine Tudor.

She was very proud of this name and of her country and of London; she loved London.

And she loved her dog.

She was, like so many others of her generation, shocked by what was happening to young people. She didn't understand the changes in attitudes and the new morality. To her, "permissiveness" was an ugly word. For years she had gone about her beloved Hampstead Heath worried by the shamelessness of young lovers. Where some, rightly or wrongly, kept to the beaten track, without seeing the lovers in their arbors, she went wherever the little dog led her, and iron entered her soul.

She longed to do something to prevent promiscuity and what she felt was an abuse of the public parks and commons, and when she saw in a shopwindow in Hampstead Village a handwritten poster announcing a meeting of all who wanted to clean up the parks and open spaces, she was almost the first in the church hall where the meeting was being held. Not quite the first; there were others who felt as strongly as she, and they were ahead of her.

Quite a number of the people who attended the meeting joined the E.L.C. and pledged themselves to take active steps to help clean up London. Some of them were old enough to remember and to talk about the days of Sylvia Pankhurst and the early suffragettes. All were prepared to chain themselves to railings, organize marches and meetings for the distribution of leaflets, undertake anything and everything that would contribute to the funds of E.L.C.

Geraldine Tudor joined proudly in such endeavors. When she had been asked by telephone, in the name of the local Chairman of the Committee, to go and walk her dog near Ken Wood, she had done so unhesitatingly in spite of the fog. And when she had been instructed by a woman from the organization, in a passing car, to distract the policeman, she had done so at once, thrilled to be of use.

Now she knew what she had really done.

Was this for the good of E.L.C.? If it was, she would, of course, take the consequences. But she had not been able to get any reply to a telephone call to the Chairman, and now she simply didn't know what she should do.

But her little dog must be exercised; she would decide what to do when she came back.

98

Half an hour after watching Gideon, she had left her large bed-sitting room in a big house on the other side of Hampstead Heath, the dog frisking eagerly beside her and a shawl over her arm. The common was only a hundred yards away, and she picked the dog up as soon as she was outdoors and bundled him up in the shawl. Once on the common, she would probably meet no one, and the fact that she had a Yorkshire terrier with her wouldn't be noticed.

As she left the garden, a man moved out of the shadows. She didn't notice that he followed her.

When she reached the Heath, she loosened the shawl and bent down to let the dog wriggle clear of the wool. Almost at once, he started to bark furiously. She turned round, whispering urgently, *"Quiet, boy, quiet!"* But suddenly she saw the man with his arm upraised, and in his hand a weapon, clear against the light of a lamp on the other side of the road.

She screamed.

The dog yapped furiously, and as the man lunged forward, it leapt at his ankles. The silence of the Heath was broken by a furious commotion, the dog snarling, the woman screaming, the man swearing and trying to shake himself free. Then, without warning, a powerful torch shone out. The man turned to run, but the dog held him by the trouser end. The policeman holding the torch took three masterful steps forward, handcuffs dangling from his left wrist, and as the attacker's weapon arm swung round, he grabbed, twisted, and snapped on the other handcuff.

The headlights of a police car came swaying along the road which bordered the Heath. Geraldine Tudor bent down and gripped the still furious dog, clutching him to her. The man handcuffed to the policeman stood gasping for breath and glaring, but the policeman was young and powerful, and the man's weapon—two feet of iron piping—was on the ground.

The police car stopped and two men spilled out.

"I think he was going to kill the woman," the policeman said, "but don't worry about *him,* look out for that dog. He's a spirited little basket."

"Who can I tell?" Lennie Sappo asked himself, in acute distress. "I shouldn't have been there. If I tell the cops, they'll nab me!"

12

Murderer?

"GEORGE," Kate Gideon said, "it really won't do any good to worry so much."

"I know it," Gideon admitted. He was prowling about the middle room just after half past ten that night. "All the same, I'm as worried as hell. I'm far from sure I should have mentioned the woman with the Yorkshire terrier, and— Oh, I know, what's done can't be undone, but I simply don't know what to do next. I feel as if I'm in a fog, and can't see a damned thing clearly."

"You expect too much of yourself."

"I'm not getting enough done," Gideon complained.

"You were magnificent tonight," Kate said.

"Kate," he said, stopping and looking intently into her eyes. "It doesn't matter what kind of television presence I've got. What matters is whether I get results."

"But you can't possibly expect results until tomorrow," Kate said.

He knew that she was right. From what Scott-Marle had said

to him after the broadcast, as well as from other Yard men not prone to giving praise, he knew that he had presented the situation clearly—probably as well as any man could have done. But inwardly he was agitated. He knew that the kidnapping had forced him to put into words what he had long believed; had made him suddenly articulate; had enabled him to speak for all dedicated policemen. And despite the few misfits, most policemen *were* dedicated.

Yet he wondered whether he had overdone what had to be said, whether he had jumped the gun, and convinced the kidnappers that having Hobbs would win them nothing. If that was so, had his words condemned Hobbs to death? What would Penny think? Would *she* believe he was prepared to sacrifice her beloved on the altar of principle? And *had* he been wrong to mention the Yorkshire terrier? If those who had killed the unknown man in Hobbs's car thought that the dog would lead the police to her, then obviously she was in acute danger. He was more on edge than ever; it wasn't fair to take it out on Kate, but that was what he was doing.

Into a brief silence the telephone bell rang.

He hesitated, then swung round to take the call at the extension close to the passage door. It could be news from the Yard; he was stiff with hope.

"Gideon," he said in a clipped voice.

"Daddy," Penelope said. "You were wonderful."

He caught his breath; and then waved to Kate, so that she could take the call on the kitchen extension.

Penny went on: "I hated what you had to say but I know you had to say it."

"Bless you." His voice was gruff.

"Penny," Kate said, "he's been flagellating himself because of what you might think."

"Oh, nonsense! Daddy, you mustn't." Penelope's breathing was coming more quickly and her voice almost faded; why was it that there were some moments which broke down all barriers, bared all feelings, brought buried tears close to the surface? He could actually hear her gulping. "Is there—is there any news?"

"Not yet," Gideon said. "The moment there is—"

"I'm sorry to interrupt you," a woman said briskly, "but I have an urgent call for Commander Gideon from Scotland Yard. Will you take it now, sir, or shall I ask them to call back?"

Gideon answered quietly, "One moment, please, and I'll take it. Penny, what's your telephone number in Liverpool?" He took down the number she gave him, and went on: "If there's any good news—any news at all—I'll call you."

"All right." Penny sounded as if tears had caught up with her.

Gideon was quiet only for a moment as his daughter hung up; then he said to the operator, "I'll take that call now."

It seemed a long time coming through, so long that Kate said into the extension, "Do you think they've found him?"

"Don't know," he replied, and thought, Alive or dead.

Then Sharp, of K.L. Division, spoke in his unmistakable voice, putting some fears and some hopes at rest: "Commander, we have the woman and her Yorkshire terrier. We also have a man on a charge of attempting to cause her grievous bodily harm. He was about to attack her with an iron bar of a weight and shape which could have been used to kill the man in Mr. Hobbs's car."

"I'll come over," Gideon said at once. "Have you questioned them yet?"

"The woman seemed to be near a state of collapse—if it hadn't been for her dog, she might have been killed. The man won't talk."

103

"We might find a way to persuade him," Gideon said. "Are you checking his fingerprints against any found on the car and in that garage?"

"Yes—as fast as we can," Sharp told him.

"Good." Gideon put the telephone down and moved into the middle room as Kate appeared from the kitchen. He was aware that he was going to leave her alone; she must be very lonely these days. He was surprised to see that she was smiling.

"I'm sorry—" he began, and then had an idea. "Would you care to come over to Hampstead? I'm not likely to be there long."

"No, George, I shall be perfectly all right," she replied. "If I don't call the children, they'll call me; they've probably tried and found the line engaged. You be as long as you have to be," she added, and suddenly her expression changed and was almost as bleak and ruthless as his could be at times. "Find Alec, whatever you do." They stood face to face for a moment or two, and then she said, "I never did have much doubt about how much she loved Alec. Now I've no doubts at all."

"I'll find him," Gideon said gruffly.

The man who had been stopped from attacking Geraldine Tudor, first by the terrier and then by the police, was hard-faced, hard-eyed. If there was such a thing as a criminal type, he was it.

He refused to give a name, had nothing in his pockets or on his clothes to identify him.

"Who sent you to attack Miss Tudor?" Gideon demanded.

They were in the cells beneath the divisional station; Sharp was with them, a sergeant and a police officer in the passage; the cell door was locked.

The man didn't answer.

104

Gideon said, with an outward show of mildness, "You still have a chance to turn Queen's evidence. You may not have another."

The man returned his gaze impassively.

Gideon said, "You must know that your employer will send someone to kill you to stop you from talking, as readily as he sent you to kill Miss Tudor."

The man did not change expression, or move, or speak.

"All right," Gideon said to Sharp. "Charge him with attempted murder and have him up before the beak first thing in the morning." Laying a hand on Sharp's shoulder, he went on: "You're sure the piece of iron this chap had was roughly the same size and weight as the one which was used on the man in Hobbs's car?"

"As sure as I can be," Sharp said.

The prisoner said with harsh triumph, "You won't find any blood on it."

Slowly, Gideon turned round.

"Then let us have your suit."

"Why the hell should I?"

"Because I say so. If you haven't started in thirty seconds, I'll send for a couple of men to strip you."

"But *why?*"

"Have you ever heard of a blood test?" Gideon asked him. "It's a simple and foolproof one. If there's a single speck of blood on your jacket or trousers, we'll know in half an hour whether it was the dead man's or not."

The man said in a high-pitched voice, "I didn't kill anybody!"

"Are you going to take off your clothes or are we going to have to take them off you?"

Very slowly, fearfully, the man began to undo his tie. Gideon nodded and turned round, motioning the turnkey to open the cell door. He held it wide open for Sharp to pass through, and the prisoner made a wild rush, pushed him aside, got out of the cell and into the passage, and then ran into a blow from the sergeant's enormous fist.

"Keep at him," Gideon urged Sharp. "He'll crack. First he'll remember his own name and then with luck he'll begin to remember others."

"That's the way I want it," Sharp said.

Gideon nodded, and went upstairs, first to see P.C. Best, then Geraldine Tudor.

He recognized the elderly policeman he was seeking without difficulty.

"Are you P.C. Best?"

"Yes, sir."

"You saw the old lady and her dog last night?"

"Yes, sir." Best began to go pink in the face. "Proper fool she made of me, too."

"You escorted an old lady who seemed lost in the fog to where she told you she lived," Gideon said. "I hope any officer would do the same. It would be nice if we all had a built-in lie detector, but we haven't."

"Well, *I* haven't," admitted Best woefully. "And that's a fact."

"How often have you seen her tonight?"

"Twice, sir."

"You're absolutely sure she is the same woman?"

"I'd give up my pension if she isn't," Best said, with such comical confidence that Gideon was surprised into a laugh, and there was a general chuckle from everyone nearby.

"All right," Gideon said. "I'm going to talk to her. Come in, and make yourself inconspicuous. You may have to remember most of what she says."

106

"I'll remember," Best assured him earnestly. "Don't you worry about that, sir."

Gideon opened the door of the waiting room where Geraldine Tudor sat. She was sitting back in an easy chair, the dog in her lap. A plainclothes policewoman sat at a small table, an open notebook in front of her, a paperback book also open, to one side. At sight of Gideon, she sprang up.

"Good evening, sir."

"Good evening," Gideon said. "May I see your notes, please?"

"They're in shorthand, sir; they wouldn't mean anything to you, but—but Miss Tudor's hardly said a thing."

"I see." Gideon looked at the elderly woman. "Have you checked whether she needs anything? Tea, coffee, cigarettes, or—"

"No! No! Poison all!" cried the woman distractedly. "I don't know what the world is coming to when even the police shrug their shoulders and do nothing when our parks are used as brothels and places of assignation!"

The dog started barking furiously. A fringe hung over his eyes, yet they shone brightly; the long hair on his back seemed to dance like silver waves.

"Madam," Gideon began, taking advantage of a lull. "Madam—"

"I know who you are! I saw you on television only tonight, you—you *hypocrite.* You talk like that because a friend of yours has been kidnapped, but what do you do about the *thousands* of people whose whole lives are in jeopardy in our parks? Dens of iniquity, *that's* what they are, and you let your men ignore it, absolutely ignore it. *Hypocrisy!* That is the only word —don't you talk to me, Mr. Gideon! When are you going to

107

save London? That's what I want to know. That's what all decent people want to know!"

She stopped, glaring.

The policewoman stood by the table, looking at the old woman as if mesmerized, and P.C. Best, on Gideon's other side, regarded her openmouthed. When her voice stopped, the dog yapped, but she covered its muzzle gently with her veined and brown-spotted hand, and it settled, curling about in her lap again.

Gideon spoke in his gentlest voice.

"I understand exactly how you feel, Miss Tudor. In fact, that's what I've come to talk to you about."

The rage died out of her eyes and she relaxed; once relaxed, she began to shiver.

13

A Name to Begin With . . .

GIDEON WENT to the table and pulled out an upright chair. Standing close, he would tower frighteningly over Geraldine Tudor, and one way or the other she had been frightened enough.

"There is so much to clean up, some of it obvious, some of it under the surface," Gideon said. He was like a father talking to a child. "And we shall never do it if we don't work together."

She rubbed her eyes.

"I know how impatient you, and many others, must feel," Gideon went on, "and I know how easy it is to make mistakes when one loses patience."

She breathed: "Impatience? We've waited so long, so very long."

"Yes," Gideon said, "but now you've brought yourself in conflict with the police. With authority. So we have to spend time arguing—quarreling—with you, when you want the same things that we want."

"You—you even break up our meetings," she protested, with a brief return of spirit.

"Yes, I know. But we have to keep the streets clear. Miss Tudor—do you think I could talk to your leaders?"

She drew her shoulders up defensively.

"Why should you?"

"Because I think we should work together," Gideon repeated quietly. "You know it won't get us anywhere to be on opposite sides." When she didn't answer but continued to look at him suspiciously, he went on: "Now, I'm sure you were asked to mislead Constable Best here for a very good reason. Unfortunately it took him away from his duty—his actual work on the beat—at a time which proved to be very serious. Do you know why you were asked to mislead him?"

She muttered, "No, no, I don't."

"You were asked to, weren't you?"

"I've sworn an oath of allegiance," she declared, with a flare of pride. "I don't question my instructions, Mr. Gideon. I simply obey."

"Most praiseworthy," Gideon said. "Have you had many such instructions?"

"I am *very* active in E.L.C." She spelled the letters out meticulously. "And I *often* have to distract the police."

"Indeed," Gideon said, and smiled at Best. "No wonder you were misled, Constable! We are dealing with an expert." Best had the sense to say nothing and Gideon looked back at Geraldine Tudor. "Can you give me an example?"

"I'm not sure that I should."

"Oh, just a general example, not a specific case," Gideon said reassuringly.

"Well, perhaps I could do that," she conceded, and she began to stroke the Yorkshire terrier with long, smooth movements. "If we are to hold a meeting, or to clean out some—

some cesspit of iniquity, I will distract the police or park-keepers while the task is carried out. I consider it my duty," she went on proudly.

"I am sure you do. Just as I consider it mine to protect public property."

"To protect these licentious young animals, you mean!"

"If I can do the one without the other, I would be very glad," Gideon declared. "Did the request yesterday—"

"It was not a request, Commander. It was an instruction from a senior officer."

"And you obeyed just as my men would obey," Gideon mused. "Did your instructions yesterday come from the same source as they usually come?"

"Naturally they did."

"Whom did it come from?" asked Gideon, and shifted his chair in the hope of distracting her from the significance of the question.

"My superior, as always," the woman said primly.

"Do you know her?"

"I knew her voice, Commander, and that is sufficient for me."

"Ah," said Gideon. "You identified the voice of a superior. Are you sure it was—"

"I am not in the habit of making mistakes," Geraldine Tudor asserted with great severity. "Nor am I so easily fooled as you appear to think. It was apparent from the beginning that some of our actions would be unlawful—just as the actions of the suffragettes were unlawful. But they succeeded as ours will succeed." She drew her shoulders back proudly as she went on: "We have a very efficient organization. We do not give instructions by name; we learn the voices of our superiors whenever we are to receive instructions which may be unlawful. So we cannot betray our leaders."

111

Gideon pursed his lips before he said, "Very clever, Miss Tudor; there are some very astute minds behind this. However—" He let the word hover in the air.

Best shifted his position. There was a sound at the door, but no one tapped and it didn't open. Gideon stood up very slowly, his height and girth dominating the room. It seemed a long time before he came to a standstill a few feet from the woman.

"Would your leaders connive at murder, Miss Tudor?"

"Most certainly not!"

"Yet murder was done."

"I had no part in it, and neither did they."

"I don't for a moment suppose you did—wittingly."

"What do you mean—*wittingly?*"

"I mean it is easy to imitate voices," Gideon said with quiet vehemence. "And if someone used the voice of your superior to make you distract a police officer while a serious crime was being committed, then you would not be responsible in law, but morally you could not evade some measure of responsibility." He moved still closer, and went on in a husky voice, "Could you, Miss Tudor?"

The old lady did not answer.

"Nor could your superior," Gideon said. "And cold-blooded murder was committed. Moreover, had the police not arrived in time, you might well have been murdered yourself tonight. So your superior's moral responsibility is much greater than yours. And if her voice could be imitated so as to deceive you, then it could be imitated to deceive others. I must talk to your superior, at once. What is her name, please?"

"I—but I don't know!" the other gasped. "That's the whole idea."

"You must know some of the leaders in E.L.C.," insisted

Gideon. "You didn't become an active member without meeting others, learning the rules and regulations. To whom did you swear your oath of allegiance, for instance?"

"Lady Carradine," the old lady answered dreamily.

It was apparent that the moment she uttered the name she had misgivings. Her lips puckered, and she drew her body together as if she were suddenly cold. The vital thing, Gideon knew, was not to show his own satisfaction; to conceal from her the fact that he had been working up to this snap question ever since he had started talking.

"I think I know Lady Carradine," he said musingly. "I'll have a word with her myself—or, better, get the Commissioner to have a word with her." He studied this woman, wondering what to do with her. If they kept her here, it might be a kind of disgrace from which she would never recover; on the other hand, she seemed to live alone.

There was a tap at the door, and the policewoman came in carrying a tea tray with cake and biscuits, and a bowl of minced meat for the terrier. I'll leave her here and let them look after her, Gideon decided. He was on edge to get away. He smiled warmly at Miss Tudor, gave the terrier a tentative pat, said "Good night—and thank you," and went out. A door farther along the passage was open, and he heard Sharp's voice on the telephone. He needed a little time to digest what he had learned from the woman, but it would be better to finish with Sharp, then get home; or he might indeed go to Scott-Marle's home.

Sharp was saying: ". . . you might have to go in the box, you know. . . . All right, if you're as positive as that, I'll tell the Commander." There was a bang as the telephone went down, and when Gideon stepped into the doorway, Sharp was getting up from his chair behind a flat-topped desk. His expression was unmistakably one of excitement.

"Got him!" he exclaimed.

"The man downstairs?"

"Yes! There is a section of his right-hand forefinger tip on the weapon used to kill the man in Hobbs's car; and two prints of his little finger on the steering wheel. Don't know about his clothes yet, the report isn't in."

"And his name?" asked Gideon.

"If he's got a record, we'll soon know it." Sharp dropped back into his chair. "How did you get on, sir?"

Gideon told him.

"My God," said Sharp. "I knew these Elsie people were pretty quick off the mark, but this is real organization. Do you know this Lady Carradine?"

"Slightly," Gideon said. "She's a well-known do-gooder and organizer for charity and social and community affairs." Hobbs would know her, he thought fleetingly. *Where was Hobbs? Was he alive?* "Keep the name Carradine under your hat," he went on to Sharp, "and tell Best and the policewoman to do the same. Can you put the old lady up for the night?"

"We'll fix something," Sharp said. "Don't want her charged, do you?"

"Not at the moment," Gideon said.

He thought, but didn't say, that it was possible Geraldine Tudor had fooled him. There was no way of being absolutely sure yet.

It was half past twelve when he was driven away from the police station, and he had to decide what to do.

Call Scott-Marle? There was a case for it; the Commissioner was on the same social footing as Lady Carradine—as was Hobbs. On the other hand, he could go and see her himself, and talk to her before consulting Scott-Marle. He *could* wait until morning—nonsense! Quite suddenly he knew what to do. Learn what he could about Lady Carradine, and then call on her. First, call Scott-Marle and tell him about the man they'd arrested—*no*. Check if the man was known to have a record.

There was no traffic to speak of and soon they were at St. John's Wood.

Suddenly, Gideon leaned forward and said to his driver, "Take me through Regent's Park."

"Right, sir."

Only the main gates were open, but that didn't matter. A few lovers were still snuggled in the backs of cars; two couples were walking across the grass.

"Pull in here," Gideon ordered, and the driver did so. Gideon took the walkie-talkie off its hook, and Information answered almost at once. "I want all you can give me on Lady Carradine in the next ten or fifteen minutes. Her address—"

"40 Adderley Terrace, sir, Regent's Park," Carpenter, the man on duty, answered. "I happen to pass there on my way home most nights. She—" He broke off. "Sorry, sir."

"No—what were you going to say?"

"My wife's a great believer in her, sir. She's done some wonderful work for women's causes, family planning, and so on. My wife's on a local committee."

"A local committee of what?" asked Gideon, and held his breath, expecting to hear "E.L.C."

But the man replied, "The Women's Emancipation League —a kind of down-to-earth and less revolutionary women's movement, sir. Lady Carradine is the president. Is that the kind of thing you want, sir?"

"It is. Check *Who's Who* and read me what it says about her when I call next," Gideon ordered. "Now I want to talk to Sir Reginald Scott-Marle."

"Just a moment, sir—oh, there was a message from him earlier, to the effect that he would be out until after midnight, but it's past that now."

In a few moments, Scott-Marle's voice came through, distorted but understandable. "Is there any news of Hobbs?"

"No," Gideon replied, "but we've arrested a man who will probably be charged with the murder of the man found in Hobbs's car. He won't talk, but he may when he knows we have enough fingerprints to damn him." Gideon decided then to mention Lady Carradine in passing, and he went on without a change of tone: "He was about to attack the woman who distracted the attention of the policeman at Hampstead."

"So you've got *her,* too."

"Yes," Gideon said. "She's a member of the group known as Elsie. I'm on my way to see a leading member of that group now, Lady Carradine. Can you brief me about her?"

Scott-Marle didn't answer at once. In fact, the silence lasted for so long that Gideon wondered whether he should have mentioned the woman, after all. He heard the atmospherics, saw a couple drive off in a car a few yards away, yet another walking slowly across the grass. This, on a night when the temperature was down to freezing.

At last, Scott-Marle replied: "Yes, I can. She is a second cousin of the Home Secretary, a great social worker, and a great puller of strings. She is also a convinced believer in women's rights, and she will undoubtedly attempt to impress and influence you by a recital of her social and political associations. I need hardly advise you not to be influenced," Scott-Marle added dryly.

"I'll try not to be," promised Gideon, relieved by the other's approach.

"Let me know during the night if you've word of Hobbs. Otherwise we'll talk in the morning. Good night."

Gideon rang off more slowly than his chief, and very thoughtfully. Scott-Marle had told him a great deal in a few words and, characteristically, had not asked him why he was going to see Lady Carradine. It was as well to know what to expect. She would probably be resentful at being visited so late; she might even try to put him off.

He said to the driver: "Number 40 Adderley Terrace."

"Right, sir."

"Did you get a snack at Hampstead?"

"Yes—I'm good for all night, if necessary."

"I hope it won't be," Gideon said.

Five minutes later, the white porticoes of the houses in Adderley Terrace loomed up in the darkness. Gideon got out, and walked up several imposing steps bracketed by two massive pillars.

But before he rang the bell, the door opened.

Hilda Jessop, strikingly lovely in the half-light, stood in the doorway.

14

Lady Carradine

HILDA WAS OBVIOUSLY as startled as Gideon.

After a moment, when he had recovered from the surprise, he decided that she was more than startled; she was frightened.

She held the door tightly, and Gideon deliberately waited for some seconds before he said, "Good evening, Miss Jessop."

"Good evening." She was breathing quickly. "Can—can I help you?"

"Can you tell me where to find Alec Hobbs?" She started, quite visibly.

"What? What a ridiculous question to ask!"

"It's a question I ask everybody," Gideon said flatly. "I want to see Lady Carradine, please, on an urgent matter."

"Lady—Carradine?"

"Yes, at once, please."

"But—you can't."

"Why not?"

"She's in bed."

"Unfortunate, but it can be rectified," Gideon said, in a no-nonsense voice. He moved forward, and Hilda Jessop stood aside, making no attempt to stop him. A single wall light cast a slanting glow over oil portraits and dark furniture. Once he was inside, he asked pleasantly, "This isn't the address you gave at the Yard this morning, is it?"

"No, I—I don't live here."

"Are you a friend of Lady Carradine's?"

"Yes. We—we work together."

"On this work you discussed with me this morning?"

"Yes," answered Hilda, and Gideon thought she was relieved by the turn of the conversation. "Commander, can't this business wait until morning?"

"I'm afraid not."

"Lady Carradine went to bed *very* tired."

"I won't keep her a moment longer than I must," Gideon said. "The sooner I see her the quicker I'll be gone."

"Yes, I suppose so," Hilda said. "I'll go and see if she's awake." She turned and started for the stairs.

After a quick look round for something more comfortable, Gideon resigned himself to a carved-oak chair. He was becoming accustomed to the dim light, and took note of the fact that the paintings, four portraits, were of great quality. Everywhere was a sense of luxury; well, there would be in all of these houses.

Where had Hilda Jessop been before he arrived?

Had she been standing looking out of a downstairs or a first-floor window? They were positions from which she could have reached the door when she had; but of course it was just possible that she had been about to leave. He was not sure that it mattered; what did matter was her nervous manner and her attempt to save Lady Carradine from being interviewed.

119

She had certainly been badly shaken when he had asked whether she could tell him where to find Alec Hobbs.

Was it conceivable that E.L.C.—

His train of thought was interrupted by a movement upstairs; and another light was flashed on, a chandelier. It shone just above and yet behind Hilda Jessop, and the effect was quite astounding. Her suit glittered a silvery color; her blond hair seemed to be filled with lights, too.

She called, "Lady Carradine will see you, Commander. Please come up."

He went up slowly, ponderously, and yet with his heart beating faster than usual, keenly aware of the rare beauty of this young woman. She did not move until he was halfway up the stairs, and did not look away from him. It was almost as if she were trying to hypnotize him: all outward signs of fear had left her. He was aware of her physical presence, and also aware of a question that gradually grew more persistent and compelling. How could a man like Alec Hobbs be impervious to a woman of such beauty and background? He pictured Penny beside her, then pushed the thoughts away angrily. He wasn't here on Penny's behalf; he was here to find the Deputy Commander, quite sure that unless he found him quickly there would be an ultimatum from his captors—an ultimatum that could lead to disaster.

Hilda went ahead of him; everything about her scintillated —clothes, eyes, hair. She motioned toward the front of the house with her left hand; it was a slim hand with slender fingers, and ringless.

How could one separate personal hopes, longing, emotions, and fears from one's work? He was not two men but one. "One man in his life plays many parts." The same man played them; one was always oneself.

He was aware of perfume; he was sure she had put it on since she had opened the door for him. Now she pushed open a door that must open onto a room overlooking the terrace, and called in her bell-like voice, "Commander Gideon is here." He went in with heavy and deliberate tread, wanting to be thought of as a flatfoot; a man with no imagination.

Lady Carradine was sitting up in a huge carved bed.

She was a heavy-featured, heavy-breasted woman, and her wrap of pearl-gray silk was loose about her shoulders and held very loosely at the front. Temptingly? She had a long, narrow face, which looked odd above that full body. Her hair, almost the same color as the wrap, was loosely brushed and had a feathery effect; here was a combination of young woman and old—almost an elderly coquette. Yet there was nothing coquettish about her blue-gray eyes, which held both purpose and determination.

"Diana, Commander Gideon—" Hilda began.

"I am acquainted with the Commander," Lady Carradine interrupted. "We met on two—or was it three?—occasions some years ago."

"Two," Gideon said. Outwardly he showed no surprise; inwardly he was astonished that she should have remembered. "Lady Carradine, this evening a woman was detained on suspicion of helping in the conspiracy to abduct my deputy, Mr. Alec Hobbs. She stated that she did so on instructions from a senior officer in the E.L.C.—of which you are a leading member. Were you aware of what the woman was ordered to do?"

The reply came quickly: "I was not."

"How absurd," interposed Hilda, in a voice which was only just audible.

"Nothing absurd about it." Gideon swiveled his gaze toward her. "She stated that she has often been given instructions to distract police officers from their duty. Is that true, Lady Carradine?"

There was even the possibility, Gideon reminded himself, that Geraldine Tudor had lied.

But this time Hilda Jessop made no comment, and the older woman looked at him very directly as she said, "Yes."

"That is a dangerous practice, and—"

"Oh, nonsense!" interrupted Lady Carradine. "For some ridiculous reason, the police have decided to persecute the harmless but very earnest members of a group which has the worthiest of objectives. The police have to be outwitted, that is all. It is surprisingly easy, Commander. I am sure the general public would be appalled if they knew how easy; and I am equally sure that some of my very good friends in Fleet Street would be glad to give the details ample coverage."

"Such as Jefferson Jackson."

The woman's eyes had a wary expression.

"I have no idea whom you mean. I do not deal with reporters; my influence is with the papers' owners."

"Lady Carradine," Gideon said, "there is no lawful reason why I should not make a statement, including your involvement, in—"

"I am *not* involved."

"You have admitted involvement with an organization which makes a practice of lying to, and misleading, the police in order to hold public meetings in places where they are forbidden. You—"

"I would never have believed a man in a position of authority could be so pompous!"

"I would never have believed a woman of such distinction and background would behave with such indifference to the law. I have some questions to ask you—are you going to answer them truthfully or not?"

"I shall do what I wish in my own home. Let me remind you, Commander, that a police officer has no right to interview anyone without another officer present. And in doing so you are most ill-advised. Both Miss Jessop and I can testify to your aggressive—indeed belligerent—manner, and I do not propose to be badgered by you on any pretext."

There was more than a touch of satisfaction in her voice, and out of the corner of his eye Gideon saw the smile of satisfaction on Hilda Jessop's face. More, he was quite sure that the older woman was in earnest: the two of them could, and under provocation would, corroborate any story.

He said pleasantly, "Let me put you right on the facts of life, Lady Carradine. A police officer is completely free to do what he thinks best. What he can't do is use as evidence anything said to him if he is alone when it is said. As to any wisdom, Ma'am—I have succeeded in satisfying myself that my informal approach was a waste of time, and that I must be much more formal. I require you to come with me to Scotland Yard for questioning." He saw how utterly astounded the women were, held Lady Carradine's gaze for a few tense moments, and then strode to the French windows which opened onto a balcony overlooking the park. Had Hilda been there when the car had driven into the private road?

He stepped outside and called down: "Davies!"

The driver was standing by the side of the car, reading an evening paper by the light from a porch. He peered up.

"Sir?"

"Have a car sent round with a woman officer," ordered Gideon. "Then come up and join me here. The front door's open. Turn left at the head of the stairs; you'll see the open door."

"Yes, *sir!*" called Davies, just loud enough for Gideon to hear.

Both women must have heard Gideon's instructions. He waited only long enough for Davies to take the radio-telephone off its hook, then strode back into the room.

Lady Carradine's voice, when she spoke, had lost its vibrancy. She appeared to have some difficulty in getting the words out.

"Ask your questions, Commander. I will answer them if I can, and they can be answered as well here as at Scotland Yard."

Stonily, Gideon said, "Right. I will make a start here. Whether we go to Scotland Yard will depend on your answers and how freely you give them. Did you give instructions to Miss Geraldine Tudor to distract a policeman while he was on duty yesterday afternoon? And if you didn't, do you know who did?"

Lady Carradine did not answer immediately, but cast a swift, alarmed look at Hilda.

Then she said, "To the first question—no, Commander. To the second question, a qualified 'no.' I do not know who gave her these instructions but I might be able to give you some assistance. You see—" She drew a deep breath, and Gideon had no doubt at all that she was deeply worried; whether she was about to tell the truth or not there was no way of telling. "I have trained a number of the members of E.L.C. to implicit obedience. I have trained them to accept without question the need to mislead the police. They, as well as I, feel completely justified, Commander. However, I have of late had reason to believe that someone *not* authorized has been giving them orders. That this weapon has been turned against us. Geraldine Tudor was almost certainly a victim of this trickery."

Gideon asked coldly, "Do you mean trickery, Lady Carradine? Or treachery?"

On that word, the driver Davies came into the room, so quickly that Gideon was sure he was bursting with news.

He did not wait for orders to speak, but cried, "There's been word from Mr. Hobbs, sir! At the Yard!"

15

Treachery?

GIDEON HAD SCHOOLED himself over the years to be ready for the unexpected; to watch other people's reactions while concealing his own. He had a picture of the stolid driver's excited face, and then he turned toward the women. Lady Carradine's expression was one of complete surprise, while Hilda piously ejaculated, "Thank God!"

Davies suddenly realized that he may have been too impetuous; that it might have been a mistake to make the announcement in front of the women. In some circumstances it could have been, but in these, Gideon decided, it didn't greatly matter.

"What else?" he asked.

"He's going to call again, sir, in half an hour's time, then every half-hour until he gets you. He—" Davies gulped. "He's under duress, I understand."

"So I would expect." Gideon pondered, then went on with great deliberation: "I can't be at the Yard half an hour from now. I—" He looked at a telephone by the side of Lady

126

Carradine's bed and moved toward it, asking with mechanical courtesy, "May I use your telephone, please?" She said, "Yes," or at least formed the word. He did not pause until he had the receiver to his ear, and was dialing.

After a moment he said, "Gideon. Who took Mr. Hobbs's call? . . . Let me talk to him." He held on for the last man he had expected, and indeed would have wanted: Superintendent Nathaniel Bruce. "Bruce, exactly what did Mr. Hobbs have to say?"

He listened for a moment, and then looked at his wristwatch.

"I can't be back by then, and I don't want to miss him. Have him call this number if he can, will you?. . . One moment." He read aloud the number on the telephone disk: "Hampstead 851712. . . . Yes, I'll be here. . . . Is there anything else? . . . All right, thanks."

He rang off and rubbed his chin, as if at a loss for words. But he wasn't at a loss; he knew exactly what he was doing and saying, even when he spoke a little above a whisper, as if he were talking to himself. "Except that he is being held captive but being treated well, he would only say he had to talk to me."

He fell silent for a few moments, and then shook his head, as if out of a reverie.

"Davies, when that car arrives—I think I can hear it—send the woman officer up here; and have the others wait downstairs. You wait for me, too." He nodded dismissal; then, moving back to the window, he said in a clear, carrying voice, "Now, Lady Carradine. How long have you been training your members to this kind of civil disobedience?"

"For some time," she replied.

"Weeks? Months? Years?"

"Years." There was stubborn defiance in her manner but

she had lost much of her confidence. Gideon's task now was to get the information he needed without deflating her too much; it was never wise to destroy a woman's ego completely.

"On what scale?"

The woman police officer came in, but Gideon didn't think the woman in the bed realized it; he wasn't so sure about Hilda Jessop.

"On whatever scale I felt necessary to draw attention to the scandalous behavior of young people in the parks."

"Lady Carradine," Gideon said, "there are a lot of people who would think permissiveness of sexual affairs, brazenness, and what you would doubtless call licentiousness preferable to any attempt to break down the forces of law and order."

"You are exaggerating what I did out of all proportion—" Lady Carradine began, but she stopped even before Gideon actually spoke, as if she anticipated his reaction and his interruption.

"You have created conditions which have apparently enabled other criminals to commit a very grave crime indeed. That is not exaggeration." He shot a glance at Hilda Jessop, asking sharply, "How long have you been aware of this?"

"I—I told you this morning."

"And you didn't know before?"

"No," Hilda Jessop answered. "I had no idea. I knew how strongly my aunt felt"—Gideon tried not to show his surprise at the revelation that these two were related— "and I knew she organized the protests, but I didn't think she actually organized the—vandalism, the destruction. She has been a great help in my society, and—"

"Hilda," interrupted Lady Carradine, "I don't know *what* makes you think that *I* took any part in the destruction of the bushes and shrubberies."

"Didn't you?" demanded Gideon.

128

"Most certainly I did not."

"Then who did?" Gideon asked.

The woman in the bed closed her eyes for a few moments; she began to speak before she opened them, as if she felt this was a burden too great to bear.

"I don't know who did, Commander. I do know that some of the E.L.C. workers have been instructed, without my knowledge and I am sure by no one in my organization, to distract the police, park-keepers, and others while the damage has been done. If I knew who—if I even suspected who it was —I would tell you. I must ask you to accept my assurance that I have no idea at all."

Again Gideon looked at Hilda.

"Have you, Miss Jessop?"

"No," she answered. "I have no idea. Alec—Mr. Hobbs— told me he suspected that the vandals and the civil-disorder organization were one and the same. That's what he really wanted me to find out. Commander—"

"Commander." Lady Carradine's voice rose over the younger woman's. *"You* have to find out who has used our organization for this destructive reason, and why—"

She broke off abruptly, for the bedside telephone rang; and instantly the name of Hobbs sprang to Gideon's mind. He moved forward and had the receiver to his ear before the bell had given two double rings.

"Hallo, Alec," he said, so sure that it would be Hobbs.

"But I'm not Alec, Commander," a man said, in a voice which had a curious, hollow-sounding echo. "But I shall cut his throat, or have his head bashed in, if you don't call off your dogs."

The voice was speaking through some thin substance placed over the mouthpiece, which added to the savagery of the threat, to the horror it caused. In spite of exerting every effort he was capable of, Gideon almost lost his self-control, almost cried out in protest.

Teeth clamped together, he said, "If you have any sense at all, you will release Mr. Hobbs at once."

The "Mr. Hobbs" had a strangely archaic, artificial sound. He was aware of that, and of the man at the other end of the line; not of these two women, or of the third one at the door. For a split second, he thought he had broken through the other's guard; but almost at once the man laughed, and went on laughing. It was forced laughter, but there was something hideous about it. For the first time, Gideon wondered whether he was dealing with a sane man.

At last, the other said, "You make me laugh, Commander, you really do. *You're* the one who needs the sense. If you've got any, you'll call off your dogs; otherwise you won't have Mr. Hobbs to hold your hand or sleep with your pretty daughter. I'll give you until tomorrow. Just tomorrow, that's all. By tomorrow night or—"

Across his words there came an earsplitting scream: *"No, don't!"*

Gideon felt his heart thudding, felt the horror of helplessness, expected the telephone to be banged down; but instead there were background noises—laughter, voices, a snatch of music.

Into this, Hobbs's voice came quietly: "That wasn't me, George."

Gideon's throat felt stiff and painful.

"I didn't think it was."

"I'm sorry I've got you into this mess," Hobbs went on.

"Got *me!*" said Gideon.

"Well, you are in a mess," Hobbs said. His voice was quite normal and controlled. "I wish to God I could do something to help, but even if they would let me talk I couldn't tell you anything of significance. I don't know where I am or who is responsible for the kidnapping."

"Are you all right?"

"Yes," Hobbs said, and actually managed to laugh. "There's a woman here who cooks stews better than most, and her dumplings—" He broke off, only to say in a different, harder tone of voice, "George, don't do anything they say."

Gideon didn't speak, but the other man spoke with the mesh still over the mouthpiece.

"You'd better do everything, Commander."

"George," said Hobbs, "if the situation were reversed, I would not allow myself to be blackmailed into any course of action. Give my love to Penny."

"I will. Alec—"

"That's enough," said the man with the distorted voice. "Keep away from those parks, Gideon. Draw off the dogs." He gave the laugh again but rang off in the middle of it, and the receiver went down noisily.

Gideon stood absolutely still for what seemed an age; he was oblivious of the others in the room, and his mind was working with a speed that only emergencies could stimulate. The other three remained as still as he.

When at last Gideon moved, it was slowly; when he spoke, it was mildly.

"Lady Carradine, I shall leave two police officers here, and I'll be glad if you will make a full statement of what you have told me. It will be typed and ready for your signature by ten o'clock in the morning. Add any details—or matters of significance—which you may have forgotten. For your own safety, I shall have a guard placed on this house day and night until this business is over." He turned from her to Hilda Jessop.

131

"Miss Jessop, I would like you to come with me, please. There are some matters on which you can help." He nodded to Lady Carradine and crossed to the door.

Outside, he talked to A.B. Division, which included Regent's Park, arranged for the statement to be taken and the house to be watched, and by that time Hilda Jessop had joined him; she now wore a dark coat, with a chiffon scarf tied over her hair.

"If you will ride with these officers, they will follow me," he said.

"Where are you taking me?"

"To Scotland Yard."

"Am I under arrest?"

"Miss Jessop, if at any time I think you should be arrested, I shall leave you in no doubt of it." He opened the door of the other car for her and she got in the back seat; an officer sat beside her. Gideon went back to the large car, and as Davies took the wheel, he said sharply, "The Yard—as quick as you can make it." He lifted the receiver from its hook as they started off, and Information answered almost as if someone had been standing by for his call. "I want this message to go to all divisions and subdivisions," Gideon went on. "They are to have a detailed report ready by noon tomorrow listing exactly what measures they are taking for security in the parks and open spaces. How many men are involved, when it began, how many instances of vandalism and/or arson have been reported, how many known to have been checked."

"Right, sir." This was the man who passed 40 Adderley Terrace so often on his way to work. *"Is* Mr. Hobbs all right?"

"So far," Gideon said tersely.

"Is that all, sir?"

"No." Gideon paused again; the only sounds were the atmospherics and the whir of the tires. Abruptly he went on:

"Another paragraph. Mr. Hobbs is held in a house in which there is an extension to the telephone. All divisions should contact their telephone manager's office and check where telephones with at least one extension have (a) recently been installed, and (b) are installed in houses which were empty until recently and where the telephone service might have been restored after a period when it was not operative. Have you got that?"

"Yes. Shall I read it back, sir?"

"No, have it typed—I haven't finished yet—and sent up to my office. I'll be there in twenty minutes. I'll check it before it goes out. Add another paragraph. There are at least two men and one woman in the household where Mr. Hobbs is being held. One man has a phrase he used often and may use again—'draw off the dogs,' or 'call off your dogs.' I have no information about the other, but the woman is apparently a good plain cook. The fact that she cooked dumplings was mentioned."

"Shall I put that in, sir?"

"Yes. Any suspicion, no matter how remote, that individuals might be known or identifiable should be reported to me at once; my office will be available day and night. *Special note:* No steps of any kind should be taken without prior consultation with the undersigned. George Gideon, Commander, C.I.D." He paused again, and then was caught by a huge yawn, smothered it, and added: "That's the lot, Carpenter."

"Right, sir."

Gideon sat back and closed his eyes—and Hobbs's voice seemed to echo in his mind. Every word and every nuance was deeply etched, and Gideon began to search afresh for any hint that Hobbs had tried to give him. He could see none except the mention of the woman cook.

Echoes grew louder:

133

"George, don't do anything they say."

"You'd better do everything, Commander."

"If the situation were reversed, I would not allow myself to be blackmailed into any course of action."

"Give my love to Penny."

"That's enough. . . . Keep away from those parks, Gideon. Draw off the dogs."

The words and the voices merged together. Gideon was aware of movement, of drowsiness, of words and faces that were confused, and then of a cessation of the movement, making him open his eyes. Davies was looking at him, as if commiseratingly, and they were outside the Victoria Street entrance to the Yard.

"There shouldn't be so many pressmen here, sir," said Davies, getting out.

"No," Gideon said. "Thanks." He got out, with Davies's hand on his elbow. "You get off home, Davies. I shall probably put my head down here for a few hours."

"I do wish you would, sir!"

"I almost certainly shall. Good night."

"Good night, sir."

Gideon went into the nearly deserted hall; only Hilda Jessop and one policeman were there; the driver must have gone off. It was overwarm, and the woman had loosened her coat. Gideon nodded, and said to the policeman, "Arrange for tea and coffee and sandwiches in my office, will you?" Then he led Hilda to the lifts. "I can do with a snack and I daresay you can." She didn't speak, and they reached the second floor and went along to his office, passing Hobbs's. He felt an ache behind the eyes, probably because he was hungry. He opened the office door and was startled to see a man sitting in his chair, with files in front of him.

It was Superintendent Bruce, as immaculate as ever. He

rose quickly when he saw Hilda, and obviously did not know what to say. His mouth was actually open as he looked from one to the other.

"Superintendent—Miss Hilda Jessop."

"Good evening, Miss! Commander, so many messages have been coming in I thought someone should be in your office. I—"

"Quite right. Is there anyone in Mr. Hobbs's office?"

"Yes, sir—a man taking any messages that might come in."

"Good. You might tell him to call the canteen and ask them to make that order for three people," Gideon said. "Sit down, Miss Jessop." He rounded his desk and placed his heavy coat on a hanger that Spruce Bruce was quick to take from a wooden clothes stand. "Superintendent, there will be a draft of a general call up here soon. I want to read it before it's sent out. It might help us to trace Mr. Hobbs."

"Did you actually speak to him?"

"Yes." Gideon looked levelly at Hilda as he answered, then went on: "I want Miss Jessop to answer some questions and it would be useful if we had notes of them."

"I'll take 'em," Spruce Bruce said eagerly.

"Very well. Miss Jessop, did Mr. Hobbs tell you anything about the inquiries he was making—what he was doing, who was involved?"

"No," she answered.

"Is there anything about his discussions with you that you haven't divulged?" Gideon asked.

She didn't answer.

"Miss Jessop," Gideon said earnestly. "I think you have a deep personal regard for Alec Hobbs. Have you?"

Her lips hardly opened as she answered: "Yes." And, with the word, thought of Penny cut through Gideon like a knife.

16

Empty House

"YOU'VE KNOWN Hobbs a long time?" Gideon asked the woman.

"Yes."

He could only just hear Hilda Jessop's word.

"Since childhood?"

"He was—older than I. I was a—child, yes."

"Did he ever return your—deep regard?" Gideon asked.

He saw Bruce's hand pause for a moment, knew that the man looked up from under his lashes. He saw Hilda close her eyes as if she were suffering from an unbearable headache.

"I don't see what this has to do with—with the situation," she said.

"It could have a great deal to do with it," replied Gideon. "A policeman is first a man. A man might conceivably bend rules and regulations for someone with whom he was in love, for instance, or with whom he had once been on terms of intimacy. Were there any special circumstances which might justify Alec giving you special—even privileged—treatment?"

After a long time, she answered, "Only—friendship. He—he has never returned my feeling for him."

"I see. Thank you. Did he give you privileged treatment?"

"No," she said. "No, I don't think so. He—he told me he couldn't. He *did* say there were things he could keep to himself for a while and might never have to disclose—they might prove irrelevant. But I think he would have said as much to any woman in trouble."

"What trouble *are* you in?" Gideon asked gently. "You told me, and you told Alec, that you thought your life was in danger. Do you really think so? Or did you say this simply to win sympathy?"

She spoke very, very quietly: "I think I am in danger."

"From whom?"

"I don't know."

"Do you know why?"

"That was what Alec was trying to find out."

"Did you tell him all you could?" asked Gideon, and when she didn't answer at once, he went on in a firmer voice: "Did you tell him everything, or only part of what you knew or suspected?"

Slowly, painfully, she replied: "I didn't tell him everything. I—I couldn't understand why my aunt was involved in this—this vandalism. I've known her organization for some time, and have tried to find out what possible reason there could be. *She* says someone else is using it for their own ends, but—I'm not really sure that's right. I'm afraid she might be more deeply involved than she will admit. I—I am frightened in case it is *she* who is threatening me, in order to stop me making inquiries. I went to her house tonight to face her with this. She denied it, but I am still not sure."

Hilda broke off, and Gideon watched her for a few moments before asking, "You didn't tell Alec of these suspicions?"

"No. I simply said I would try to find out. But don't you see what could have happened? If my aunt—if whoever is involved—found out I was seeing Alec, they might think I'd told him much more than I had. *That* might be the reason he was kidnapped. If he is murdered, then it could be because I didn't tell him all I knew."

As she spoke, tears sprang to her eyes. Gideon had little doubt of the depth of her love for Alec Hobbs.

He was glad when there was a tap at the door and a messenger came in with the tea and coffee and sandwiches. Almost at the same time his general call was brought in. He altered a word here and there and let Bruce read it, then sent it back signed. It would reach all divisions within half an hour.

Twenty minutes afterward, he said to Hilda, "We can find you a comfortable chair in which to spend the rest of the night, or we can see you home, whichever you prefer. Superintendent Bruce will get you to sign a copy of what you've told us in the morning."

"I would prefer to go home," she said.

"Very well. Will you arrange it, Superintendent? And also arrange for a close watch on Miss Jessop's flat—for her own protection."

"I'll go with her," Bruce volunteered eagerly.

"Miss Jessop," Gideon said. "You have nothing to fear from the police, provided you have told us the truth."

"I have," she assured him. "Everything."

But had she? He wondered.

It was half past four. Despite the ache at the back of his eyes, he didn't feel particularly tired after Bruce and Hilda Jessop left, and his mind was alert. He had one quick decision to make: whether to rouse Scott-Marle and report that short distressing conversation with Alec, or to wait until the morning. But in his own interests, as well of those of the case, he ought to get some sleep. He had done everything that could be done; the yeast would not begin to ferment until the morning, when the Force had time to study and think about his message.

He gave a wide yawn.

I'll go upstairs, he decided, and went to the door of Hobbs's room. It was strange to see a youthful-looking detective sergeant there instead of Alec. "I'm going up to the dormitory," he said. "Call me if there's anything urgent."

"I will, sir."

Gideon nodded, went back to his room, and stared at the reports on the desk, then picked one up. It contained a summary of the messages that had come in during the day from people who claimed to have seen Hobbs. Twenty-one of these came from the Hampstead area and each had been closely checked. Eighteen had been discounted; two remained open.

One said a woman had reported that a man answering Hobbs's description had been pulled out of a black van by a man and half carried by some women into a small house that had been for sale for several months.

The second said a youth had reported seeing a black van being driven too fast through the fog, half a mile from the spot where Hobbs had been kidnapped. On both was a note: "Statements being checked."

Why wasn't I told? Gideon complained to himself. That house ought to be raided. He put in a call to Hampstead and was not surprised to find that Sharp was still on duty.

"My fault," Sharp said apologetically. "I should have told you. We checked, and the house is empty. It's been sold to a couple who are moving in next week."

139

"Any telephone?" asked Gideon.

"Let me see," Sharp said, and paper rustled. Then, in a tone of surprise, he said, "Yes. A main instrument in the front hall downstairs and an extension in the back room upstairs. It was owned by an accountant who used the upstairs room as an office."

"What are the approaches like?" asked Gideon.

"It's at the foot of a high railway embankment," Sharp replied. "No way of approach without being seen. Only one road goes past it, but this road links up with a corner of Cricklewood Lane, and a T-junction at the other; one bar of the T leads to Cricklewood Lane, the other's a dead end."

"Looks as if they knew what they were doing," Gideon said. "Jack, have that place watched every minute of the day and night. Don't make any move but make sure we know everyone who goes in and out."

"You can't think—" Sharp began, but broke off.

"Like extra help?" asked Gideon.

"I can look after it," Sharp said, and rang off.

Gideon, sitting on the corner of his desk, stared at the big round clock on the wall. All sense of tiredness had left him. The discovery, if it *was* a discovery, had come out of the blue, almost out of nothing. No lead-in, no build-up, almost an anticlimax. *My God!* Now he *had* to call Scott-Marle!

He put out a hand for the telephone, but as he placed his fingers on the instrument it quivered, then rang. He let it ring for a moment. If Hobbs was in that empty house, what were the odds on getting him out alive?

The bell kept ringing.

The door from Hobbs's room opened and the sergeant said, "Just checking you're still there, sir. Would you like me to take the call?"

"No, I'll take it." Gideon lifted the receiver stiffly. "Gideon."

"Daddy," said Penelope, "is there any news?"

Her voice seemed far away, and frightened. "Daddy, is there any news?" There was news—what the devil was the matter with him?

"I couldn't sleep," Penny was saying, "and I rang Mummy. She said you might be at the Yard. Daddy, *is* there any news? I'm on the way back. We'll be in London in two hours."

"I have talked to Alec," Gideon said. "He's being held as a hostage, but he's well and they're feeding him."

"Oh, thank God! I was afraid—"

"Penny, they won't kill Alec unless they're sure they can't get what they want," he said.

"They mustn't kill him!" she cried. "You mustn't let them!"

"There isn't a thing I won't do to save him," Gideon promised her. At the back of his mind there was a hazy realization that there were some things he could not do, but all he could think of at that moment was the distress in his daughter's voice.

"You mean that?" she cried. "You really mean that?"

"Penny—" he began.

"You've got to mean it!"

"Penny," Gideon said. "Go straight home. Would you like to be met anywhere by a police car?"

"No, my friend will take me right to the door."

"And I'll come as soon as I can, with all the news I can," Gideon promised. "I can't stay now."

"I know," Penelope said huskily, but she didn't ring off and he just caught the words that followed, and he could almost see the tears. "I can't live without him—"

141

Then she rang off.

Gideon put the receiver down slowly, painfully. He put his hand against his forehead, and it was burning hot. He had much more than an ache behind the eyes now; he had a headache that was spreading like fire. He had a sense of disaster. It was probably because he was so emotionally involved in this affair.

He had intended to call Scott-Marle, but was it really necessary to wake the Commissioner to report that he had talked to Hobbs? He moved from the desk to the window. It was a clear night and the lights on the Embankment, on Westminster Bridge, and on the far side of the river were all very bright, calm, and clear.

He moved in sudden decision, and picked up the exchange telephone. "A line, please, and leave it through." He dialed Scott-Marle's number, and the bell rang four short double rings before the Commissioner's voice sounded, blurred by sleep.

"Scott-Marle."

"Gideon, sir." Gideon paused long enough for the sleep to clear from the other's mind before going on: "I've talked to Alec. He's all right so far. His captor's first demand is that we withdraw our men from the parks and commons by sunset tomorrow. I was noncommittal. I have also talked to Lady Carradine, and there is no doubt that she is partly responsible for what happened—wittingly or not, I don't yet know."

"Be sure before you take any action," Scott-Marle said.

"I'll be sure," answered Gideon gruffly. "It's possible that we know where Alec is being held. I'm having the place watched from a distance, but I'm taking no action yet. I would like to discuss it with you tomorrow."

"At whatever time you wish," the Commissioner agreed. He showed no sign of excitement; he was a master at concealing his feelings. "George, what made you say, 'His captor's first demand'?" Sleep-heavy or not, his mind was alert enough.

"I can't believe that all they want is freedom of the parks," Gideon answered. "Unless—"

"Unless we are dealing with a fanatic," remarked Scott-Marle.

"Or, more likely, unless there's some reason why he needs the parks," Gideon replied. "I simply can't think of one. I'm still at the Yard, sir. I think I'll go home for a few hours, but I'll be on call if there is any development."

"Try to get some sleep," urged Scott-Marle, and rang off before Gideon could reply.

Sleep, thought Gideon. Sleep. But Scott-Marle wasn't emotionally involved; it was difficult enough to rest and relax, and might well be impossible to sleep. But he must go home; he needed a talk with Kate before Penny arrived, and there was nothing he could usefully do here. Once again he went to the door of Hobbs's room.

"Changed my mind," he said. "I'm going home. Have a car ready for me, will you?"

Ten minutes later, he was on his way; twenty-five minutes later, he let himself into his house. He went upstairs slowly, surprised at the heaviness of his legs. The dining-room clock struck six. Penny would be home by seven, perhaps earlier; it wasn't worth going to sleep until she came.

He went into the big bedroom.

The light was on, but Kate was asleep, breathing evenly. He couldn't wake her. When it came to the point, all he wanted was to be here when Penny arrived. The job he was on now was terribly important, but he had to be here for a while, to help Penny. He took off his shoes and loosened his collar, then slumped into an armchair.

143

He was bodily weary, but mentally so alert that he didn't think for a moment he would go to sleep.

But he did sleep, through the sound of a car stopping, through the opening and closing of the front door, through Penelope hurrying up the stairs, through Kate waking and Penelope crying and Kate trying to soothe and to quiet her. It was Penny whose voice finally pierced sleep, made him suddenly awake.

"I tell you I don't care, I don't care! He must wake up. He must do what these devils want! He must save Alec's life!"

When Gideon opened his eyes, he saw her standing in front of him, young, pretty, and full of fear. Kate was behind her; he knew that she was pleading with him, wordlessly, to help Penelope: to put their daughter above all else.

17

Father and Daughter

SLEEP STILL held to him, tightly. It chained and locked his body, and befogged him. He shifted his position; there was a pain in the back of his neck and an ache in his head.

"Father! Wake up! Listen to me!"

"Penny—" Kate began.

"Mother, be quiet! This is between Father and me." Penelope leaned forward and gripped his hand in both of hers and tugged, trying to get him to sit upright. "You must save Alec!"

Gideon said: "Hallo, Penny. I must have dropped off—"

"How you *could* sleep when Alec's in this awful danger and I'm beside myself, I don't know!"

He struggled to a sitting position at last. She held fiercely to his hand, her eyes glassy and deeply shadowed. He remembered all that had happened, her call from the motorway; the mists of indecision cleared.

"Yes, my dear," he said. "You are certainly beside yourself."

"Anybody would be in these circumstances!" Her voice was high and overwrought. "Alec might be killed, murdered, and you don't care, you just come home and fall asleep in an armchair. How heartless can you be?"

Gideon looked at her for a long time, considering half a dozen different phrases before he replied in a voice that held a core of hardness. What he said had to be right: for himself, for Kate, and above all at this moment and for all the future for Penelope. He phrased his words with great deliberation.

"If Alec could see and hear you now, he would be ashamed of you. You are no longer a child: you are a young woman of twenty-six, with all an adult's responsibilities. Accept those responsibilities, Penelope, or the day will come when instead of crying that you can't live without Alec, you will find that you can't live with yourself."

"George!" Kate said.

He didn't look at or respond to her, not wanting to join issue with her. He looked instead at Penny, longing to draw her to him and to soften his voice, knowing that at the moment he dared not. He had been afraid after the telecast that she would take his attitude badly, and had been enormously relieved when she had phoned him. What had made her change? Had she simply brooded and brooded, not sleeping for the torment in her mind, and found it grown into a nightmare that rejected all reason?

Or—

Suddenly, he thought he knew the reason.

For a moment he was sick with himself because he had not seen the obvious quickly enough, but gradually he realized that it was as well that he hadn't, because he couldn't have brought himself to talk as he had if he'd even suspected the truth.

She released his hand, and turned away, burying her face

against her mother's shoulder. Kate looked at him; and he hadn't seen such coldness in her expression for many years.

She said firmly, "I'm going to give her a sedative and put her to bed."

"Not yet," said Gideon, "there are one or two things I have to know."

"She's at the point of exhaustion!"

"Yes," agreed Gideon, unable to keep the weariness out of *his* voice, "I know. Penny, did someone telephone you and tell you that if I didn't do what he wanted Alec would be murdered?"

Kate said, "No!"

Penelope's head rose quickly. "You knew?"

"I guessed," he said. "Sit down, love." He reached for her hand. "Penny, has Alec talked about this case to you very much?"

"A little," she replied.

"Does he usually talk about investigations going through at the Yard?"

"No, hardly ever." When Gideon waited, she went on: "This one worried him much more than most."

"Did he say why?"

"No, except—" Penelope fumbled at the neck of her dress and drew out a damp-looking and crumpled handkerchief. "Except that he didn't really think it was simply a 'clean up our parks' motive. I think—" She hesitated, and when she spoke again, her voice was much stronger. "I think he was afraid that there were political undertones."

Gideon asked sharply, "Did he ever say so?"

"No, but—well, I couldn't imagine any kind of crime that would worry him so much," Penelope answered. "But I'm only guessing."

"Did he ever mention a woman named Lady Carradine?"

147

"No. The synthetic Women's Lib Lady C.?"

"You could say that! Or a Hilda Jessop?"

"No."

"Anyone at all by name?" Gideon asked.

"Only someone named Elsie," answered Penelope.

"It isn't a someone, it's a code name," Gideon said rather grimly.

Penny looked at her father with great intentness before she spoke. "How odd. But that could explain why Alec often talked about her with exasperation, couldn't it? Or frustration. He always said he could be sure when she would turn up— it was whenever he needed to concentrate on another, more important job."

Slowly, Gideon said, "What job?"

"He didn't say what it was."

"Penny, try to remember," Gideon said urgently. "Try to remember exactly what he said about Elsie and another job— or jobs."

"Job," Penny insisted.

"Always the same one?"

Penny's eyes were beginning to blaze, and she answered eagerly, excitedly, "Yes, I'm sure of that. Alec said there was just one major case he wanted to crack, and just as he was on the point of doing it, Elsie distracted him. I thought he was really talking about a woman. Daddy! Have I helped? Have I?"

"You might have helped more than you'll ever realize," Gideon told her. "Kate, get me some breakfast, will you? I'll have a quick bath and be on my way. Penny, call the Yard and have them send a car for me, there's a pet."

"In half an hour?"

He nodded.

Penny turned and hurried down the stairs. Kate, retying her

dressing gown, said, "George, I'm—" He crossed to her with a startlingly swift movement, slid his arm round her, and kissed her.

"Think Penny will be all right now?"

"Yes, I think she will," Kate said, smiling. "We both know you'll do whatever you can."

He thought, But what will Penny—what will Kate—do and feel if I have to sacrifice Alec?

Alec Hobbs was sleeping fitfully in the bed in which he had first come to. His wrists were again strapped to the framework.

In the next room Clara was in a double bed with the man who had menaced Hobbs with a gun; she was snoring faintly.

Downstairs, the man who had spoken to Gideon was talking on the telephone, an electric fire drawn up close to his feet. His teeth, as he spoke, chattered from the cold.

"I want to know whether we're being watched, that's all. If we are, we've had it. I'll cut Hobbs's throat and get away. . . . If we haven't been spotted, then we still have a chance. . . . I'll let you know," he finished with a note of exasperation in his voice, and banged down the receiver.

The *ting!* sounded loud in the silent house. It woke Hobbs, but he didn't know what had disturbed him. He began again to try to loosen the straps; but it was impossible. These people had him absolutely at their mercy.

What did they want?

Gideon turned in to his office at half past eight feeling much less tired than he had any right to expect. He looked into Hobbs's room and found a different man there taking messages. He grunted good morning as the man stood up.

"Mr. Sharp says, will you call him, sir."

"Get him for me and put him through."

149

"Very good, sir. I've made a list of everything that's come in during the night, sir."

"Thank you." Gideon went back into his own office, and looked through the files; there was nothing significant yet, as far as he could judge. His telephone rang and he thought it would be Sharp, picked up the receiver, and said, "Don't you need sleep?"

"Who, me?" It was Lemaitre, in a bright and lively voice. "Slept like a top, George. I've gotta bitta news for you."

"Lem, unless it has to do with Alec Hobbs—"

"Well, it could be," drawled Lemaitre tantalizingly. "It has to do with a dame who ran a little caff in my manor. Know what everyone called it? The Dump—how about that? Add a 'ling' and Bob's your uncle. Got it? Lived with a man—common-law husband, as a matter of fact—who did odd jobs with a van, mostly furniture removals."

"A black van?" Gideon broke in.

"That's the one he was running last time I saw him. We had him inside once—had a habit of moving furniture that didn't belong to him. Name of Barrow—Syd and Clara Barrow."

"Do you know where they are now?" asked Gideon.

"No, I don't. But they're Londoners, wouldn't go far from the big smoke. Want me to put out some feelers?"

"Yes," Gideon said, "but very cautious ones, Lem." He slackened his grip on the telephone, his hand numb from the tension. "We think they're holding Alec Hobbs, and I'm afraid they might kill him and try to get away themselves if we get too close."

"I'll be cautious all right," Lemaitre promised. "As a matter of fact, there was a load of furniture taken out of a shop on the Mile End Road last week. We'll say we're looking for Syd because of that."

"Keep in close touch," Gideon said. "Thanks, Lem."

150

He rang off, his heart thumping. "A little caff in my manor
. . . The Dump—how about that?" There was a beading of
sweat on his neck and forehead. It wasn't certain; he was doing
a Lemaitre, jumping to conclusions, but—

The bell rang again; this would be Sharp.

"Gideon."

"Good morning," Sharp said, in his most incisive manner.
"I don't think there's much doubt that place in Cricklewood
is the one we want, sir. We've found a lad who saw a black
van go up to the front door. If Mr. Hobbs was there last night,
he's certainly there now."

18

Demand

"Quite sure?" asked Gideon.

"Certain. It's an easy place to watch—to get away from it you have to pass one of two corners. I've got men inside houses on those corners, and I've men on the roof, too."

"For God's sake, don't let them suspect for one moment that they're being watched," said Gideon earnestly. "It could be fatal."

"I'll see to it. Anything happened I don't know about, sir?"

"Lemaitre thinks he might have identified the woman who makes dumplings. Her husband runs a furniture-delivery business, using a black van. That's about the lot."

He rang off, wiping his damp forehead with the back of his hand, then looked with great deliberation through the folders that covered the major cases under investigation. He had to make himself realize that the Hobbs affair wasn't the only one. He telephoned five Superintendents and two Chief Inspectors, men whom Hobbs would usually see before Gideon briefed them. Two had made arrests, the others had nothing new to report. Probably nothing they wanted to disturb him with now, he thought.

Then he called Bruce's office.

Bruce might not be in yet, of course; he hadn't finished until the small hours. But he answered the call on the first ring, and was as brisk as ever.

"Superintendent Bruce."

"Come along and see me, will you?" Gideon said.

"I'm on my way!" It was possible to believe that Bruce was actually springing from the desk as he put the receiver down. Gideon pushed all the other files to one side and took out the jewel-robberies file, which was fatter than most; he thumbed through it with one hand as he dialed Scott-Marle's office on the interoffice telephone. The Commissioner answered almost as quickly as Spruce Bruce had.

"Good morning, sir," Gideon said. "This is—"

"Good morning, George. What is the situation now?"

"We think we know where he is," Gideon said quietly. "In fact, we're pretty sure. At the moment I've kept it very quiet. The place is watched but the occupants don't know that."

Gideon paused long enough for Scott-Marle to say, "Go on."

"I think we may be close to finding out what it's all about, sir. I—"

"Will an hour make any difference?" the Commissioner interrupted. "I've a conference I really should attend."

"An hour might help me, sir."

"Very well. And, George—"

"Sir?"

"I rely on your judgment absolutely," Scott-Marle said. "If you have to take any action, take it." He did not add, but he meant: "I shall back you to the hilt."

"Thank you." Gideon replaced the receiver as there was a

sharp tap at the door. "Come in," he called almost in the same breath, and Spruce Bruce came in as if he were being pushed by some uncontrollable force. He had a file beneath his arm, but at first Gideon saw only the man, the slicked hair, the waxed mustache, the small but regular features, the bright eyes, the beautifully tailored suit, and the many-hued tie. Once or twice before, he had been aware of what he saw behind this front: a tremendous eagerness to please . . . or to succeed?

"Good morning, Commander!"

Gideon waved to a chair and said, "Good morning, Spruce."

He had never used this man's nickname before, and didn't quite know why he did then. He saw the flash of surprise in the other's eyes and wondered whether he had been wise, whether Bruce would begin to be overfamiliar. "Get anything more out of Miss Jessop?" he asked.

"No, she didn't say a word," Bruce replied. "But I've the conversation between you typed out in the form of a statement. Shall I have a copy sent to her for signing?"

"Yes," Gideon said. "Have you done any thinking about it?"

"Take it from me, I have," the other man declared. "Commander—" He broke off; behind his eagerness he was as nervous as a man could be. "Commander, *my* job has been the jewel robberies. Mr. Hobbs wished me to concentrate on those, and very rightly, but—I can't help thinking the jewel robberies and the park troubles overlap."

"What makes you think so?" asked Gideon quietly.

"Well, Commander—we've *never* found where the jewels are taken after the robberies. *Never*. None of them has ever turned up in England—not as far as I know, anyhow, and I'd know if they'd been officially reported. But twenty-seven have

154

lately turned up overseas—in the United States, Australia, South Africa, New Zealand, Canada—in the English-speaking countries, mostly. But you know that, sir—it's all in your file."

"But I may not have realized the significance of it," Gideon said.

"How do they get there, sir? By post? That is most unlikely. By air cargo? Surely improbable, sir; some of these jewels have been of fabulous value. I don't believe they would have been sent out of the country by either of those methods. I think they would be sent by special messenger, *and* by people who might reasonably be expected to have valuable jewelry with them. Do you see what I'm driving at, sir?"

"People like Miss Jessop," Gideon said.

"Exactly! I am not for a moment accusing Miss Jessop. There's no evidence. But she does travel to and from South Africa by air frequently. And she is a member of an organization many of whose members travel widely and frequently. As I begin to see the situation, Commander—" Bruce hitched himself even farther forward in his chair and peered into Gideon's eyes as if willing him to accept this theory. "The jewels are taken to prearranged places in the parks. The nearest parks to the scenes of the crimes. The thieves leave them —buried, I imagine. This park then becomes the scene of a protest march. Acts of vandalism are then carried out under cover of which the jewels are removed. *That* is why we never find any trace of them through the usual underworld channels." Spruce Bruce began to pace the room; he was just a little too graceful for a man, his suède shoes a little too elegant. "The more intently I look at this situation the more convinced I am that Elsie—a collective name, as it were—works with the thieves. Some knowingly, some unknowingly. Who would dream of suspecting them?"

"You," Gideon said. "And the Deputy Commander."

155

"But only after a great deal of thought and many false theories," said Bruce. "Commander!" He placed both hands, small and beautifully manicured, on the desk. "I have come to the conclusion that the two *are* associated. My mind has been working very fast since Mr. Hobbs was abducted; it was a rare stimulation. Against this I am faced with a terrible dilemma. How can one *seriously* suspect a woman of Lady Carradine's background and reputation?"

Gideon said thoughtfully, "What inquiries have you made about Lady Carradine?"

"A very few, sir. The Deputy Commander was quite insistent that I should concentrate on the burglaries. And since Superintendent Norton went off duty, the divisions have been in charge of the park troubles—I believe Mr. Hobbs has been correlating all the reports himself."

"Yes, he has," Gideon said. "I take it you have all details of the robberies listed up to date."

"Every robbery, every piece of jewelry, everything in chronological order, sir, and I've brought a copy in case you would find it useful." Bruce drew back from the desk and picked up his file, opened it and took out a sheaf of foolscap papers, pinned together. He placed these before Gideon with a flourish. *"There,* sir."

"Thank you. Take three or four men, and telephone each division to get the dates of troubles in local parks and open spaces," Gideon ordered. "We must eliminate the possibility of mere coincidence."

"That's been done already," Spruce Bruce said with abounding confidence. "I've checked on enough to be sure of it, Commander."

"Check again."

"I will!" The Superintendent gathered up his file and darted toward the door, leaving his list in Gideon's hand.

"Hobbs," said his captor, "is there a copy of this list in your office?"

Hobbs did not speak.

"I don't want to hurt you for the sake of it," the man said, "but I'll break every bone in your body to make you talk."

Hobbs, in a chair in the bedroom, the remains of a fairly adequate breakfast on a tray by his side, made no comment at all. He looked pale beneath his stubble and his eyes were bloodshot and red-rimmed; there was a bruise on his forehead.

The man took a step nearer and raised his clenched fist.

"Answer me!"

"I have nothing to say," Hobbs replied.

He tried not to flinch as the blow came, but drew in an involuntary breath. Then the blow landed on the side of his jaw, so powerful it sent him sideways; the chair toppled and he went flying, banging his head on the floor and scraping one hand painfully along the bare boards.

"Is there a copy of this marked list?" The man bent down and struck him again, but not so savagely. "Answer me!"

Hobbs eased himself up to a position on one knee. There was a graze on his cheek where the blood was beginning to seep through, but he didn't touch it or seem to notice.

The man kicked at his face.

Hobbs dodged, flung out his right hand, caught the other's ankle, and jerked it. The man fell back helplessly, landing against the bed. Hobbs stood up unsteadily, while the man struggled furiously to rise. Hobbs picked up the chair and raised it, then moved toward the door, ready to use the chair as a weapon if his captor attacked again. He reached the door and stretched out one hand, but the door opened before he touched the handle. The man with the gun stood there.

157

"Back you go," he ordered. "Don't fight with a bullet."

The other man scrambled off the bed and rushed forward, livid; now he had a piece of iron in his hand. Hobbs made a sweeping blow at him with the chair, but it was thrust aside. To Hobbs, death seemed inevitable; this man would crack his skull, the other shoot him. He spun toward the doorway.

"Stow it, Syd," the gunman shouted. "The Boss wants to talk to him again. Stow it, I said!" He waited until the iron bar was slowly lowered, and then went on: "You don't use the right methods for a gent like the Deputy Commander—that's your trouble. He needs to be softened up a bit. He'll find the answers soon enough."

"You bloody fool—you've fed him and mollycoddled him. The only talk he'll understand is a kick in the guts and a cracked skull."

"Stow it!" the gunman repeated. "Out!" The other obeyed, looking back venomously at Hobbs. "Okay, Hobbs," the man went on. "On the bed like a good boy."

Hobbs said, "There is no point in tying me to the bed again."

"Yes, there is," said the man with the gun. "You're more helpless that way, and after getting rough with Syd, you might start trying to get rough with me or Clara—or the Boss, when he comes. On the bed."

He was two yards away from Hobbs, and the gun was just out of reach. Was it worth a try? Hobbs asked himself. If he could once grab the gun, he would have a good chance of getting out, an odds-on chance. He was tensing himself for a spring when the other moved forward and kicked him savagely in the groin. The pain was so awful that he collapsed on the instant, so great that he was aware of nothing else, just a desire to bend and bend until he could squeeze the pain away.

158

He felt a sharp blow on the head.

Even in unconsciousness, the waves of pain came through.

He did not know what time it was when he came to. He was on the bed again, shivering. He had been stripped to his short-sleeved undershirt and underpants. Propped up on the chair by the side of the bed was a photograph—of a man's head: a battered head.

On the seat of the chair was the length of iron.

And pinned beneath it was a sheet of paper with two questions printed on it in red ink: *"Is there a copy of that list in your office? Does anybody else know?"*

He shivered violently, and it was not only with the cold.

19

Bait

"WELL," Scott-Marle said, "what do you propose to do?"

He sat at his uncluttered desk in his barely furnished office, an austere-looking man with close-cut, iron-gray hair, a weather-beaten, leathery face, very pale gray eyes. He looked as if he were still an Army Commander, much more a soldier than a policeman.

Gideon said, "I need your guidance, sir."

"Not about what to do if Lady Carradine *is* involved, surely?"

"No, sir, not that," Gideon assured him. "I simply cannot make up my mind whether to do what we've been told to do, or whether to ignore the order. If we withdraw the watch from the parks, then clearly it is possible that there will be a swoop by Elsie to collect any jewels still hidden. And if we were ready to swoop back, we could pick up a great number of the people involved."

"Yes," Scott-Marle said.

160

"Hobbs would almost certainly be killed if we did that," said Gideon.

Scott-Marle didn't comment, and didn't look away.

"However, he might well be killed whether we do it or not," Gideon went on. "If we've broken the jewel gang, then"—he moistened his lips and paused, but Scott-Marle gave him no help—"then it might be argued that Hobbs didn't die in vain."

Scott-Marle said, "Yes, it could."

"There *is* another angle," Gideon continued. "It is conceivable that Hobbs could be used as a bait."

"How?"

"He may be visited by people highly placed in—Elsie."

"The suspect house is closely watched, you say?"

"Yes. I've been out this morning to see the situation for myself," Gideon said. "The house was probably chosen because of its position. We can approach only from two directions: from the main road, or from a T-junction. One of the arms of the T-junction ends at a railway embankment, the other curves around to meet the same main road. To get to or from the house, one has to pass the T-junction or the corner of the main road. That's how it is we can watch the place without being seen, and also why we couldn't make a surprise attack: each of the corners can be kept under continual surveillance from the house."

"In these circumstances would anyone important in the organization be likely to go to see Hobbs?" asked Scott-Marle.

"I think it unlikely, but possible."

"George," Scott-Marle said, in a quiet and understanding voice, "you know what you're going to do, don't you? You simply need me to give the actual word."

Gideon thrust out his aggressive chin, as if the remark had

angered him. But he wasn't angry; he simply wanted to see clearly, and he knew of no one else in the world who could help: just Sir Reginald Scott-Marle, who was so much more human than he appeared to those who didn't know him well.

"No," Gideon replied. "I don't think that's true. I think the chances of rescuing Alec Hobbs alive are very slim indeed. Even if we do what these people want, I should think he has seen enough of his captors for them to want to make sure he can't identify them in court. If there *is* a chance, it is in raiding the house. I think we might pull that off, but since the men inside have already killed, they won't suffer any further penalties for killing Hobbs. If we take them, we may not pick up anyone who goes into the parks. I think we should withdraw our men—draw off our dogs, as the man said—but be ready to swoop. We could seal every park off quickly; we would pick up a lot of innocent people, of course, but need hold only those in possession of stolen jewels—you know what I mean, sir."

"Yes," Scott-Marle said. "You think this, although once they know they've been tricked they will almost certainly murder Hobbs?"

Gideon clenched his fists. Veins stood out on his neck and forehead. It seemed a long time before he said, "Yes, sir."

"I agree with you," said Scott-Marle. "You know—" He broke off.

"Know what, sir?"

"That it's useless to make any attempt to raid the house until after the parks maneuver."

"Yes," Gideon answered. "Yes, I know, sir. That is in some ways the worst part of it. If we are to succeed, we must leave Hobbs at risk. I don't see any way out. I've been trying to. I hoped you might see what I couldn't, sir."

"George," Scott-Marle said, "you have the clearest vision

162

of any man I know. How long will it take to make the arrangements?"

"What's left of the day," Gideon said. "We'll have to leave it to the divisions who know their manors inside out. I think I'll call a meeting of Superintendents for one o'clock—two, perhaps; they'll all be able to get here by two, and if some of them have to forgo lunch it won't do any harm. Would you like to talk to them, sir?"

"No." Scott-Marle stood up, and Gideon followed suit, more slowly. "If we ever get an Assistant Commissioner for the department, he'll be able to take over jobs like these." He put a hand on Gideon's shoulder. "I don't mean 'like these' literally, George."

"I'm sure you don't, sir," replied Gideon. "And I imagine you realize that I believe Hobbs to be the right man to be Assistant Commissioner."

"It doesn't surprise me," Scott-Marle admitted. "Once this affair is over, we'll go into the possibility more closely. There is one thing I can and will do, if it will help, meanwhile."

"What's that, sir?"

"Make it known that it was an instruction from me—my decision, not yours. I know what your daughter will feel, and possibly Kate, but it's better that they are bitter towards me than towards you."

Gideon turned to face him, and Scott-Marle's arm fell to his side.

"Thank you," Gideon said. "But I think they had better know the truth. They—" He drew a deep breath. "They needn't know until afterwards, that's one thing."

Scott-Marle nodded, then opened the door.

"Mother," Penelope asked, "he *will* put Alec's safety first, won't he?"

"Penny," Kate replied, in an even voice, "you know as well as I do that he will weigh up all the circumstances and then do what he thinks he should as a policeman." When she saw the tautness at her daughter's lips and the pain in her eyes, she went on almost as if she were praying: "It may be one of the occasions when what he should do as a policeman coincides with what he should do as a father. That's what we have to hope for. Oh, my darling, my darling!"

"Commander!" cried Spruce Bruce.

Gideon, turning in to his office after the interview with Scott-Marle, felt his nerves tauten, for the man's voice, even more than usual, held that irritating quality which set his teeth on edge. Without glancing round, he beckoned and left the door open. Bruce seemed to dance along the passage and into the room.

"I've a report from *all* divisions, Commander."

"What's the result?" Gideon demanded, but the other's manner answered the question for him.

"Without a single exception, there *was* a demonstration, *or* an act of vandalism, on the day following a jewel robbery of importance. There is no doubt the two things *are* connected." He pulled a sheaf of papers from his briefcase. "I've annotated one of my own chronological reports, in case you would like a copy." This time the flourish with which he handed it to Gideon was almost too flamboyant.

"I'll study it," Gideon said. "Whom did you speak to at the divisions?"

"The Superintendents or officers in charge."

"Still got your men together?"

"Yes, sir!"

"Then telephone them again—personally, whenever you

can—and ask them to come for a briefing here at two o'clock this afternoon. They are to tell no one why they're coming, and to keep away from the newspapers." Before Spruce Bruce could speak, Gideon went on: "Arrange for the meeting in one of the conference rooms. It will be over by three o'clock at the latest. And be there yourself."

"Sure-*lee!*" breathed Spruce Bruce, and he turned and sped to the door. "One other thing, sir."

"What?" demanded Gideon.

"I think my brother would gladly arrange to have more park-keepers concentrating on the entrances. He certainly will if it's an official request, sir."

"It's an official request," Gideon said. "And a very good idea."

Now Spruce Bruce really did seem to walk on air.

Hobbs tried to ease his left arm and shoulder, but wasn't able to. Both ached where he had banged them against the floor. His temple and cheekbone felt sore, too, and he felt nausea and a memory of pain throughout his whole body.

He didn't know what he would do when his jailers came back.

He was quite sure they would torture him, but not sure whether it would do serious harm to the police case if he talked. Above all, he wanted the police to find out the truth. He didn't want to weaken the investigation in any way, but— would he weaken it, or would Gideon have caught up with the situation by now?

It was useless to reproach himself because he hadn't briefed Gideon fully. He had believed at the time that it had been the right thing to do; he would almost certainly, if he were placed in the same position, make the same decision again.

The one thing that hurt most was thought of Penny.

He tried not to think of her, just as he tried not to think of Gideon's dilemma.

Now and again he thought of Hilda, wondering whether she was involved or not; and whether Lady Carradine was; but from his position here, either way seemed of little importance.

The question that worried him most was could he hold out under torture?

And overlapping this was another question. *Should* he hold out? Would it really help?

He shifted his body an inch or two, and as he did so the door burst open; the two men who strode in must have crept up soundlessly, so that they could scare him by a sudden rush. And they succeeded: his heart thumped, and he felt sick.

They stared at him but neither spoke. The man referred to by the other as Syd picked up the photograph and studied it. Slowly, he put it down.

"Too quick," he remarked. "The poor chap hardly knew what had hit him." He picked up the printed questions, studied them as if they were new to him, and then said to his companion, "Tap his shins, Paul, but not too hard. We may want him to walk." He looked down on Hobbs with a broad, inane grin. "Ever thought how many parts of a man's anatomy can hurt, Hobbs? . . . I once read a book about the Spanish Inquisition. Wow! Those boys certainly knew their business."

The iron bar cracked across Hobbs's legs.

Directly afterward came the question: "Now, is there a copy of this annotated list?"

Hobbs didn't really know why he made his decision; he only knew that he had made it. He must not talk. If he said yes, then it might queer the Yard's pitch completely. If he said no, they would probably not believe him. The peculiar thing was that a kind of numbness came over him, so that although

166

he felt pain it was not excruciating; not unbearable.

He didn't believe he would get off the bed alive.

"You might as well talk," the man urged. "That way you won't get hurt so much. Tell me, did you know I used Lady Carradine's envoys to take the loot abroad? The poor dears were quite unaware of it, thinking they were carrying out Elsie's brand of Women's Lib. Lady C. was so sure I was in sympathy with her aims she told me how she kept in touch with allied groups overseas. . . . Oh, she's quite a woman, our Lady C.! Fingers in all the pies you can think of. . . . Take that girl friend of yours, Hobbs, Hilda Jessop. Hilda was one of a group who helped pregnant girls who forgot to get married to holiday abroad, have the brat adopted, and come back brown as a berry. There are a dozen Hildas doing that kind of humanitarian work, and I had them take little packets to friends of mine in whatever country they were going to.

"Little political messages, they thought.

"Loot, in fact. Did you know about that, Hobbs?"

When Hobbs didn't answer, the man said evenly, "Give him another tap on the shins, Syd. That might jog his memory."

Gideon looked at the men assembled in the meeting hall in front of him. He knew each face, had a fair idea of the character of each man. Some, like Lemaitre and Sharp, he knew well. Others, like Spruce Bruce, he knew only as policemen. He had talked for ten minutes, hard-voiced and to the point; and now he had finished, the briefing was done.

"Are there any questions or problems?" he asked.

It was Lemaitre who spoke first; bony-faced, lanky Lemaitre, a kind of Cockney Spruce Bruce, sporting a red and white spotted bow tie. He was over at one side of the room, isolated from most of the others.

"Question for confirmation, Commander."

"Yes?"

"We take the dogs off at four o'clock—that's half an hour before the parks close?"

"Yes."

"We don't stop anybody who goes into the park but we pick up everyone who comes out?"

"Yes."

"Everyone who walks through a park entrance gets a luminous white paint on his boots or shoes, so when they leave they can be picked up a hundred yards or more away?"

"Yes."

"Where do we search them?" asked Lemaitre.

"We shall have a plain van parked nearby, with all facilities," Gideon answered. "A man and a woman officer will be in each; there will be a screen to give privacy. All those not carrying anything that is suspect can be released."

"Do we take names and addresses?"

"Yes."

"Do we need search warrants?"

"No. At a pinch, they can be charged with loitering with intent to commit a felony if they refuse to allow themselves to be searched voluntarily."

"Okey-doke," rejoined Lemaitre. "I've got it."

No one else asked questions, but as they began to stand up the telephone on the desk where Gideon stood rang unexpectedly. Bruce, fractionally nearer than Gideon, picked it up, listened for a moment, and then cried, "Hold him on!" The single sentence shrilled through the room, and everyone, including Lemaitre, stopped in his tracks and stared.

"It's the man who's got Hobbs!" announced Spruce Bruce in a piercing whisper. "He wants to talk to you, Commander."

20

Ultimatum

EVERY MAN in that room stood like stone. Then, very slowly, Gideon took the receiver from Bruce's outstretched hand.

No one seemed to breathe as he said in a clear voice, "This is Commander Gideon."

"Good morning, Commander." It was the voice with the metallic echo: the man who had spoken to Gideon in the small hours. "I trust you have made up your mind."

Gideon said, "I have."

"Your friend Hobbs will be most interested in your decision," the man said; he sounded almost uninterested when he added, "May I tell him what it is?"

"The police will be withdrawn from the parks," Gideon said coldly.

"Well, *well*. Your friend *will* be pleased. How wise of you, Commander! You do understand that it must be for a period of twenty-four hours, don't you?"

"Yes—twenty-four hours."

"Most gratifying." There was a momentary pause before

the man said, in a harder voice, "Gideon—don't play any tricks. Don't try to fool me. If you do, you'll have Hobbs's head on a plastic salver, and it won't look pretty."

He rang off.

Very slowly, very stiffly, Gideon said to those assembled: "There is no change in our plans, but more need than ever to be careful. Is that fully understood?" There was a rumble of assent, and he turned to the main doors. He passed young men and middle-aged, all of whom made way for him.

Several of them spoke to him.

"Very sorry, sir."

"Can't say how sorry I am, George."

"Isn't there *any* hope of getting Mr. Hobbs back?"

They sensed his ordeal; each man in his own way shared it. He didn't answer but went heavily along the hall to the passage leading to his room. No one, not even Bruce, followed him. His office was exactly the same as always but looked bleak and empty. He saw a memo under a glass paperweight on his desk, but went straight to the window and looked out. It was raining, just a fine drizzle; there was no wind, but the swish of wheels over the wet roadway was very loud. At last, he went to his desk, and picked up the memo.

The man found murdered in the driving seat of Mr. Hobbs's car has been identified by the Birmingham police as a Robert Marriott, an office equipment salesman. No motive yet known. Marriott's wife has said in a statement that she was aware that her husband had affairs but has no knowledge of anyone involved, past or present. She appears to have taken a philosophical view of her husband's infidelity. Checking possible domestic motives but none suspected.

Gideon put the report down. It was something to know the identity of the dead man, of course, but at this moment it seemed insignificant. How the hell was he going to get through the rest of the afternoon?

This wouldn't do! The work had to go on, some routine, some new cases. He made himself open file after file, and stopped at one: on top was the pathologist's report on the man Prendergast, who had died after being waylaid by Sparrow Smith on the Eelbrook Common. What an age ago that seemed! The report was simple: Prendergast had died of cardiac failure, and the pathologist had added: "Almost any shock or fall could have brought this on."

Gideon made a note and placed it on top of the file for tomorrow's briefing. Smith and his accomplices might be charged with manslaughter, but he would not recommend a charge of murder. He must remember to talk to Lemaitre about Smith.

He made notes in other files: recommendations for briefing which Hobbs normally did. That set him thinking about Hobbs again, and the parks case in general.

There was one thing he could and should do: see Lady Carradine again, and confront her with this annotated list. The truth was, he didn't trust himself to talk with her.

He could, later.

He was tempted to telephone Kate, but resisted that also. He had never felt so lonely or so helpless. If only he, George Gideon, could take an active part; could go in person to confront the devils who—

He caught his breath, and after a moment said aloud but in an almost inaudible voice, *"Well, why not?"* He moved to his chair behind the desk and dropped into it, saying in a voice that was even more still and small, *"Yes, why not?"* He began to think constructively, beyond the impulsive thought, and something akin to excitement stirred in him. What would happen if George Gideon, Commander of the C.I.D. and

Hobbs's superior, went to that house in Cricklewood *by himself?* Well, what *would* happen? Wasn't there at least a chance that the men holding Alec would want to hear what he had to say? It would be useless to go in unprepared, of course; he would need something with him. Tear gas? What was he talking about? Was there the slightest chance of getting results if he went? Wouldn't it be a vainglorious effort, carried out mainly to soothe his tortured, emotional self?

He tried to shut the idea away, but it wouldn't go.

Supposing he took high explosive? Nitroglycerine, or something safer to carry but equally effective. Why not? Years —many years—ago, he had taken as big a chance simply to capture a man wanted for murder and to save the life of a girl he didn't know. The man's name came back to him: Micky the Slob. So did the circumstances: he could have been blown to pieces, together with the ship the man was on.

If he talked about this to anyone, they would shout him down.

Scott-Marle would simply forbid it. Other senior officers would almost certainly get word to the Commissioner in order to prevent it.

He must keep it to himself.

As he worked during the afternoon he felt calmer than at any time since he'd known that Hobbs had been abducted. He put Bruce in charge of an Operations Room, here at the Yard, to work in close cooperation with Information. Every arrest would be recorded, as well as everything that was found. He fully realized that there was no certainty that jewels would be brought out of the parks, but he did not think there was any serious doubt.

He would drive himself to Cricklewood.

At five o'clock, he went along to the Operations Room, two rooms in one, where Bruce was already briefing the men who had worked with him all day. Bruce sprang up and began to show Gideon exactly what he planned.

Gideon showed a proper interest, and then said, "Exactly where is this Cricklewood house?"

"Just here, sir." Bruce had maps on the walls, showing the parks and open spaces in green, railways in red. Gideon had seen all this at Hampstead; what he had not studied was the position of the house in relation to the main roads. Bruce knew it to a square foot!

"The watch is still being kept there, isn't it?"

Bruce looked at him oddly.

"Naturally, sir—we aren't taking any chances. I was talking to Superintendent Sharp only half an hour ago, and he said no one had come in or out this afternoon."

"I'm going out to Hampstead," Gideon said. "I'll keep in touch."

"*I'll* look after things, sir!"

Gideon went out and up the stairs to Ballistics, where all kinds of explosives were kept for record and experiment. A small, bald-headed man was in charge there.

"Good evening, Commander."

"Hallo, Wilf," Gideon said, and forced a smile. "I'm having some difficulty keeping my mind occupied tonight."

"I don't wonder, sir."

"I want to refresh my mind about the different kinds of incendiary bombs recently used in demonstrations," Gideon told him.

"No trouble about that, sir." Chief Inspector Wilfred Kippen was highly gratified by Gideon's use of his first name; as gratified that Gideon should have come here to kill time. He showed specimens of the incendiary bombs Gideon had mentioned, not noticing his underlying interest in the nests of small drawers marked "Explosives."

"Good thing they haven't used high explosives," Gideon said casually.

"Some of the stuff they use these days would make a hole almost as big as Hyde Park!" Kippen joked. "Now take that stuff, for instance. . . ."

By then, the first people were being stopped and questioned outside the parks. Most were young, many were lovers, all were scared. Half were unmarried; many were married and, on that night, unfaithful. A few were defiant and even bold, and P.C. Arthur Simpson, on duty near South Park, in Fulham, had one of these to cope with. The man, carrying a parcel, objected to being taken into the mobile police station, objected to being searched.

Arthur Simpson, still flushed with this week's triumph, was in no mood to stand nonsense; and when the man refused to take off his jacket, Simpson spun him round and began to pull at one of the sleeves.

The man back-heeled so viciously that Simpson cried out in pain; only iron heel-tips could have caused such an injury. As Simpson reeled back, the man darted for the door and leapt out, sending the one policeman on guard flying with a kick in the chest. Running at great speed, the fugitive turned a corner and raced to Wandsworth Bridge Road.

The police didn't see him again.

"Won't do Simpson any harm," a colleague said unsympathetically. "If he'd found sparklers in that man's pockets, he would have been unbearable."

Simpson, blood pouring from his leg, didn't hear him. He only knew that he felt as if his leg were broken.

"It's not broken," a doctor at St. Stephen's Hospital told him. "But you won't be able to walk on that for a week."

Two or three other men escaped, but all who carried anything that looked at all suspicious were held.

The police outside the parks were at their busiest when Gideon drove off the main road toward the lonely house in Cricklewood. He knew that he was being watched, that probably word that he was approaching the house was being sent back to Sharp's headquarters, but it was too late to stop him. The headlights of his car swayed slightly as the car went over bumps in the road. Lights shone at some of the windows of the house, and Gideon thought he saw a shadow pass one of them.

He pulled up at the gate.

He got out and, leaving the headlights on, walked along the driveway. Now he saw no movement. He reached the porch, waited for a moment, then knocked sharply, a *rat-tat-tat,* which echoed for a long time.

He was aware of movements at one side of the house, and suddenly a man called out, "There's no one in the car."

"I am Commander Gideon," Gideon said, in his most authoritative voice, "and I have come alone to discuss the situation with you."

His voice echoed and re-echoed in the porch; no one replied. It was eerie standing there in the darkness, knowing he could be seen, knowing he could be shot. He stopped thinking; could only feel. Soon, very soon, he would know whether their curiosity would get the better of them.

He thought he heard a movement inside the house, and he was right, for suddenly the door was pulled open and a man rasped, "Make a false move, and I'll shoot you in the guts."

Gideon said in the same voice of authority, "I want to talk with whoever is in charge here." He was sure it was not this man with the automatic pistol; this would be Syd, common-law husband of Clara. He felt a surge of hopelessness; no one of authority would be here—

He didn't want anyone in authority: he wanted to get everyone here together, so that he could put the fear of death into them. His mood changed; and almost at that instant, a man called out, apparently from the head of a flight of stairs which Gideon could just see.

"My God!" this man exclaimed. "It *is* Gideon."

Gideon felt a sharp stab of excitement, recognizing the voice of the man with whom he had talked over the telephone.

"Yes. I am Gideon," Gideon declared.

"What the hell do you want?"

"To talk to you," Gideon said. He moved forward, ignoring the gun, and the man holding it backed away.

The one at the stairs called, "We've nothing to talk about."

"We have a great deal," Gideon said. "Tell this man to let me in."

He wondered even then whether the other would obey or whether he would be shot out of hand. He heard the labored breathing of both men, and kept quite still.

Then the man at the stairs said, "Let him in."

"It's a trap, you bloody fool!"

"He's alone. Let him in," the other insisted.

Gideon went in, taking four long strides. The man was now halfway down the stairs, a stocking mask over his face.

A woman and another man appeared at the end of the passage: Clara, of course; Gideon had no idea who the other was. The door closed behind him with a bang. He heard the gunman's surly voice snarl, "Don't try any tricks."

The man on the stairs said thinly, "Well, start talking."

"This is why I am here," Gideon said. "In my glove, and in my pocket, I have two small containers of high explosive. Each will explode on contact with anything hard. Each is powerful enough to blow this house to pieces, and everyone in it."

"You bloody fool!" screeched the man with the gun. "I warned you!"

"You're lying," said the man in the mask. "You wouldn't blow yourself up."

"I have every intention of doing so," Gideon asserted calmly, "unless you fetch Mr. Hobbs immediately, and we all leave this place."

"You're lying!" gasped the man in the mask.

"You may live just long enough to know that I am not," Gideon retorted. Very slowly he opened his left hand, with the tiny container in it. "This is the smaller of the two. Which of you will take it outside and hurl it into the grounds?" He looked coldly round at the man behind him, and said, "The other is precariously balanced. If you shoot me and I fall—"

"Oh, my God!" said the man with the gun. "He means it!"

"You're nearest the door," Gideon said, thrusting his open hand forward.

The only sound was their breathing, until suddenly the woman moved, slowly at first and then briskly, watching Gideon all the time.

She drew closer to Gideon, and said in her throaty, Cockney voice, "Open the door, Syd."

The man did not move.

"Open the door, you fool!"

Slowly, the man opened the door, and then moved away from it fearfully, obviously terrified of setting up a reverberation that might shake the capsule. The woman hesitated, then took the capsule; Gideon noticed that her roughened hand didn't shake. She moved to the door, and stepped outside; then walked perhaps twenty feet away. There was enough light to show the movement of her arm as she hurled the capsule away from her, and then turned and raced back toward the house.

Before she reached it, there was a blinding flash, a roar, and a blast that knocked her off her feet and slammed the door with a noise which shook the whole house.

When it had quieted, Gideon said, "Now fetch Mr. Hobbs."

Two of them had to carry Hobbs on the narrow bed, for his right leg was broken; but he was conscious.

The two others followed them, and Gideon brought up the rear. The group was halfway to the gate when the first police cars came tearing along the street, one from each direction. Quietly, Gideon gave instructions to the men, who did not yet fully comprehend what had happened. Hobbs was driven swiftly to the nearest hospital. The woman prisoner was put in one police car, the three male prisoners, handcuffed to each other, in another; then all four were taken to Hampstead Divisional Headquarters.

Gideon went with Hobbs, who tried to speak in spite of Gideon's "Leave it, Alec, leave it."

"What they wanted was to know whether there was a copy of the big list," Hobbs said. "They still don't know."

Soon a single hypo shot put him under almost instantaneously.

Gideon went on to Divisional Headquarters, where the prisoners were arraigned, the one man still wearing his stocking mask. "Let's have it off," Gideon ordered, and a young policeman simply gripped it at the neck and pulled it upward. Only when it was off, only when his hair stood on end and his weathered face showed, did Gideon know that the man before him was Sylvester Bruce, brother of Spruce.

"Penny," Gideon said into the telephone, "he'll be all right. He's been hurt but he'll be as good as new. He's on the way to the hospital now. I'll tell you the moment there's a doctor's report, but he'll be all right."

He rang off, looking up into Sharp's face, feeling very, very tired.

"What's the news from the Yard?"

"Seven arrests, and a total of at least a hundred thousand pounds' worth of jewels recovered so far," Sharp reported. "Bruce is dancing like a dervish, they tell me."

"He won't be for long," Gideon said heavily. "Anyone talked, do you know?"

"One of the arrested men says that the jewels were always buried in certain places known only to the thieves themselves, and collected under cover of an Elsie disturbance. He says he doesn't know the organizer, the work was always delegated, but a pattern will form, George." Sharp brushed his hand across his forehead; he was quivering. "My God!" he said. "What a thing to do. And I'll swear I'm more affected by it than you are!"

21

The Pattern

SPRUCE BRUCE looked up from the desk at which he was writing, and sprang to his feet. His expression was one of absolute triumph as he rounded the desk, and yet admiration showed through, as it did on the faces of the other men at the office, for the story had spread like wildfire. Not a man whom Gideon had passed on the way here had failed to stop and speak, or try to speak.

"Wonderful, sir!"

"Congratulations, sir."

"They must give you a George Medal, sir."

"Magnificent, sir."

And when Gideon had called Scott-Marle on the telephone, the Commissioner had said, "I don't know what to say, George. There isn't a man in the Force who won't be stirred to the heart by this. Will you come and see me, or shall I—"

"May I have half an hour, sir? I've a job to do, then I'll come."

"Whenever you like," Scott-Marle had replied.

That was behind him. Now there was this eager-faced zealot, who lived for his job, sharing in one of the Yard's greatest triumphs as well as his own.

"Commander," he said, "that was the bravest act I've ever heard of."

Gideon demurred.

"There have been plenty braver, and more remarkable. Spruce, come along to my office, will you?"

"Of course. Miller—" Bruce looked round. "Just repeat the pattern, and keep the cumulative totals going. Twenty-one arrests, Commander, and I would say that half of the jewelry stolen in the past year has been recovered. They used the parks as a warehouse!"

"So I understand," Gideon said.

Bruce, for once, fell silent, and they walked along the wide passage in an awkward silence, until Bruce burst out: "How *is* the Deputy Commander, sir?"

"Not good, but he'll pull through." They reached Gideon's office and Bruce hurried to open the door and hold it for Gideon to enter. Gideon went first to the window, then moved to the desk and sat on a corner of it, while Bruce waited, puzzled, even a little wary; it was almost possible to hear him asking himself what he could have done wrong.

"Spruce," Gideon said at last. "I don't like what I have to tell you. I don't like it at all. You know there must be a ringleader of the jewel thieves, of course."

"Surely we'll get him now, sir! I've at least six statements from accused men who almost certainly know who he is."

"We know who he is," Gideon stated. "He was at the Cricklewood house. And he was responsible for some ugly attempts to make Hobbs give him information."

"Then who—" began Spruce Bruce, only to break off and catch his breath.

181

That must have been the moment when the truth began to dawn on him. He didn't move but his features seemed to change and to become set. He was suddenly a helpless and defenseless man on whom a final crushing blow was about to fall.

"He is your brother," Gideon said, in a husky voice.

Bruce didn't shift his position; didn't look away; but he blinked several times, and then closed his eyes. When he opened them again, their light was gone.

"No—no doubt at all, sir?"

"None at all. I only wish it weren't so certain."

There was another pause. Long. Tortured.

"Thank—thank you for telling me yourself, Commander."

"Can I help," asked Gideon awkwardly, "in—in any way at all?"

Bruce's lips worked, but no words came. He turned round abruptly and stepped quickly to the window, staring out for what seemed an interminable time. He took a folded handkerchief from a side pocket and unfolded it, then blew his nose vigorously.

His voice was stronger when he replied, "Yes, sir."

"Name it."

"Permit me to carry on, sir," Bruce said, and then explosively: "Please!"

"Of course you can carry on," Gideon assured him. "I would only take you off the case if you wanted to be released."

Slowly, Bruce turned round; his eyes were red, but color was seeping back into his cheeks, and his shoulders had stiffened.

"I may want to be, later. But now I'd rather carry on." He paused, then went on quietly: "Thank you again for telling me. And—thank God you saved Mr. Hobbs!"

The best newspaper coverage, next morning, was in the *Daily Echo*. Jefferson Jackson had filled half of the front page with the story of the arrests, of Gideon's rescue of Hobbs, of the way in which the two organizations had been used. There were photographs of Sylvester Bruce, of Spruce, of Hilda Jessop, of Lady Carradine, and of Hobbs and Gideon.

A more outspoken exposé was, perforce, printed after the trial.

A pattern of events had gradually emerged, Jackson wrote.

We now know that Sylvester Bruce had for years been a receiver of stolen jewels.

He needed to find markets for them—more and more markets.

Some, in the early days, he sold in England. But as the E.L.C. organisation grew in significance, he saw another way to use it. He infiltrated their ranks with the wives of the thieves whose loot he bought.

The woman Clara is a good example of the type he used in the lower ranks.

He also corrupted some of Lady Carradine's most trustworthy lieutenants, including four who were used by Lady Carradine to give instructions to those in the lower ranks. When a demonstration in a park was planned, these women were used to distract the police and the park attendants.

It never failed.

By sending the jewellery overseas by unwitting victims who simply delivered packets for him, he received much bigger sums than stolen goods usually fetch.

One reputable member of E.L.C., Miss Hilda Jessop, took packages to places in South Africa, believing them to be political literature.

Others may well have done the same.

Two facts emerge; the first being that some of the members of the Ecology of London Committee knowingly took part in the crimes, were accessories in the selling and took part in the acts of vandalism. It will take months to find out just who was involved. Only after the most thorough investigation can the guilt—or innocence—of every member be established.

The second fact, for which we can all be justifiably proud, concerns the police, who, baffled for a while, gradually won ascendancy. Nowhere in the history of the Force can we find more outstanding examples of devotion to duty in the face of extreme danger than in Commander George Gideon and his deputy Alec Hobbs. They will be an example to the young men of the Force for many years to come.

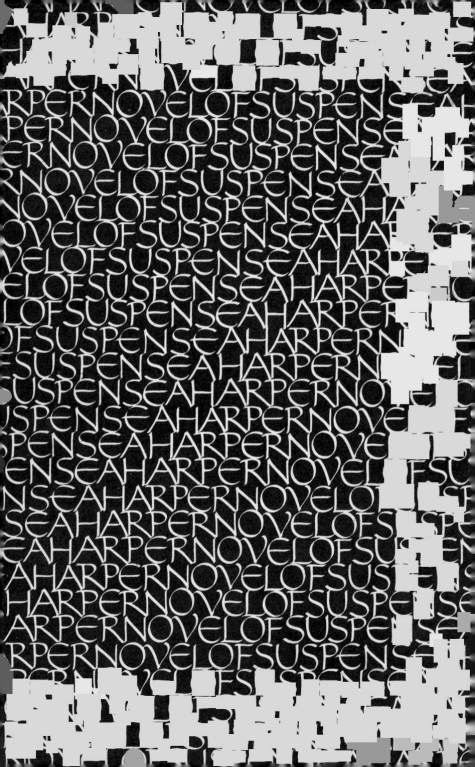